OUTSIDE

OUTSIDE

AARON GRANSBY

GERARD

First published by Gerard Books 2022

Typeset by the author
Jacket illustration: My City etching by John Duffin
Jacket design: Sean Roper
Author photography: Edmond Terakopian

ISBN: 978-1-39992907-3 (hardback)

Contents

Chapter 1

WATCHING A BUILDING ON FIRE

Rory Kennet stood alone on the Victorian iron bridge that spanned the dusty, disused road overlooking The City.

Silhouetted against the darkening autumn sky, he scanned the horizon with his grey-blue eyes before raising a pair of binoculars to his face.

The bright, artificial lights of the bewildering, mesmerising capital – effectively a nation of its own now – stretched almost as far as he could see in every direction, from east to west; north to south.

Rory breathed deeply and sought to take it all in: the high rise commercial and residential buildings fighting with each other for supremacy, a metaphor for those working and living within their walls.

After a few minutes he checked the time and focused on one spot in the west of The City. As he watched, an orange glow began to spread amid the gathering gloom. He saw the flames break through the windows of the second floor of the detached villa that sat in its own brick-walled grounds.

He knew exactly what he was looking at.

It was one of the homes of Byron St John, The City's Deputy

Finance Director; a multimillionaire businessman and one of its undisputed rising political stars.

He also knew what the blaze signified: job done.

Rory compressed his thin lips, forming a slim, knowing smile. All that remained now was for the escape to be executed – as he was sure it would be.

He remained standing on that high, narrow bridge watching the building on fire for a full five minutes, before switching his gaze once more to sweep across the broad panorama of the self-satisfied City that sat smugly within its electronic walls.

Inside, its Citizens continued to live their hard-working, hard-playing lives, paying their taxes to a government that had its own peculiar ways of keeping its non-stop, 24/7 show on the road.

It was a lifestyle that chewed you up and spat you out as soon as you were no longer of use but, while you were there, it was all you knew and, for most, all you cared about.

Rory, standing outside The City as he did now, had never truly felt a part of things when he had lived there.

As he recalled those days, which had ended so abruptly just six months earlier, he felt a sense of loss; not for the life he had been forced to leave behind, but for the life he knew he should have had instead of it.

Rory had always felt like an outsider. Now he truly was one. He had been there; he had taken part; but it had meant little or nothing to him.

Looking back, he realised that he had always seen himself in the role of the observer, the reporter... just waiting for the moment he would be found out. He had expected it to come, though not in the way it had done; when it had almost cost him his life.

His binoculars now slung around his neck, Rory's strong hands gripped the ironwork of the old bridge, and he took a step up onto the low horizontal rail, so that his head was above the top of the railings.

He felt the wind catch at his dark hair as he looked again across the vast, lit-up night-time metropolis that sprawled in front of him, so sure of itself that it seemed to dare you not to want to be a part of it.

The strengthening gusts buffeted his face and parted his hair. He could taste it on his lips, the taste of freedom.

Then, as the wind died down for a moment, he heard someone clattering up the metal steps of the bridge, followed by a shout – almost, it sounded, of despair.

Rory turned his head. A short, balding man was running towards him. He was panting a little and there was a look of concern on his reddening face.

Rory smiled.

'Are you OK?' the man asked, though he was already beginning to realise the question was unnecessary.

'Perfectly OK thank you,' said Rory. 'I was just taking the breeze and enjoying the view.'

The little man looked relieved.

'I'm sorry,' he said, 'I thought you were about to jump. This bridge is renowned for it.'

'I can see why,' mused Rory as he looked down at the empty road some way beneath him.

'It's as good a spot as any to do it, but don't worry, I've no plans to die today. There's too much to look forward to.'

The little man looked up into Rory's strong, characterful face. 'Really? Out here? You're some optimist.'

Rory smiled again, this time saying nothing. He knew what the man meant. To many, a life away from the riches of The City wasn't worth living.

Instead of answering, he held out his right arm in a flowing, slightly theatrical gesture, pointing towards the warm glow that now lit up more of the increasingly dark sky to the west.

'Have you seen that?'

'My God!' exclaimed the man. 'That looks like a proper fire!'

'Yes. It does rather, doesn't it?' said Rory.

Chapter 2

THIS CITY

SIX MONTHS EARLIER

Rory walked along the pristine streets of The City in the direction of the river. He was taking his time, looking up and around him at the buildings that shot towards the sky.

Wherever he went, something was being redeveloped.

Buildings that had been the future only 20 years ago were now the past; ground into the dust to make way for the new, to keep the economy moving and industry booming.

Today, at just after 7pm, the spring sky that Rory peered up at through the concrete canopy of the high rises was darkening and he could feel the threat of sudden, torrential rain in the air around him.

He continued walking, refusing to rush in spite of the impending downpour. He was on his way to the launch of a smart new restaurant which promised remarkable views over the Thames and incredible, if very expensive, food.

He reached his destination and walked towards the sliding glass doors. Before entering he took a deep breath, raised his shoulders and smiled. The smile was as fake as everything else in this City, but no-one other than him would know that.

'Rory Kennet, City Daily,' he said as he presented his invite at the front desk along with his coat to be put away.

'Of course, Mr Kennet, how nice to see you. Please come this way,' replied the glacial, 6ft blonde hostess with a hemline that mirrored the height of the buildings he had just been walking past.

She led Rory through into the main room of the restaurant which was already packed with people from wall to wall. As if the venue was challenging the weather to do its worst, the folding glass doors which looked out onto the river were wide open, which at least had the welcome effect of freshening what would otherwise have been a stifling atmosphere.

Rory looked around him, his smile fixed despite the cartwheels his stomach insisted on doing. He saw colleagues from the newspaper – still so-called despite it being produced digitally for as long as anyone could remember, social media stars and TV personalities, businesspeople and politicians.

He recognised many of the super-rich, including the influential Byron St John, the seemingly unstoppable politician who already held a seat on The Board – The City's appointed government – at an unusually young age.

A waiter made a sleek move in Rory's direction, offering him a glass of Champagne and a selection of canapés that looked so artistic they should have been in an exhibition. His smile still in place, Rory smoothly thanked the waiter and accepted both offerings.

The journalist certainly looked the part. His dark hair was perfect, his suit fitted as it should do and his high cheekbones and slightly too wide apart grey-blue eyes lent his features a rare character, the imperfections making the man.

But as he bit into a canapé and took a sip of his Champagne he scanned the room wishing he were almost anywhere else. He could never shake off the feeling that he didn't belong here, that he was just a watcher, not a participant.

Before he could decide which way to move, who to speak to first, he felt a hand rest gently on his right forearm and turned to see his friend, Penny Neave, standing by his side.

Her elfin face was framed by short-cropped dark hair and her green eyes looked up into his with a mixture of amusement and relief.

'I wasn't sure you would come,' she said.

'I told you I'd be here,' Rory replied.

'I know, but it's never certain with work is it? I mean, anything can happen to disrupt your plans.'

It was true; as the crime correspondent of the Daily, Rory often had to drop everything and head off, leaving others in the lurch.

'It's been quite a slow day today,' he said, acknowledging the truth of what Penny had said.

'How have things been?' she asked.

Rory looked around before replying and, seeing some people he knew just a few feet away, took Penny's arm and steered her gently in the direction of the terrace which overlooked the river, the lights illuminating the millionaires' playground of the South Bank opposite.

'We lost another one this morning,' he said quietly.

Penny looked up at him, noting the smile was no longer on Rory's face.

'Who was it?'

'Spencer Short.'

'Oh no,' said Penny. 'I like Spencer.'

Rory nodded. 'So do I. He was a really good sub-editor too. But it happened once too often. He came in looking the worse for wear and they didn't even take him into the Editor's office – the police just arrived and walked him out quickly and quietly. We were told he wouldn't be back.'

'Removed, then?'

'I don't think there's any doubt. Drink and gambling; too many problems to make him of much use anymore. It had been coming, I'm sorry to say.'

Penny thought for a moment. 'Do you think it's getting worse?'

Rory gazed across the grey river, which was looking choppy as the wind began to strengthen ahead of the coming storm.

'It seems like it. They're also getting more blatant about it. Before, people just wouldn't be there the next day. Now, like today, they simply come in and take you.'

Penny nodded. 'Talking of which, have you had any luck in finding out about Lorna?'

Rory shook his head. 'None at all – so far. I've made all the obvious checks: police, hospitals, clinics etc, but nothing. I'm going to try a few other contacts when I get home, just in case someone might know something.'

Penny looked worried. 'Please don't do too much more Rory.

I appreciate you trying but don't stick your neck out too far. I don't want you to take any risks.'

'It's fine. I can call it routine enquiries, it should be OK.'

At that moment the threatened storm struck. The sky was now black and within seconds of the first drops of rain hitting, a curtain of water fell over the river and onto the terrace. They moved inside as the rain zipped back up off the ground like bullets.

Another waiter glided towards them. This time his silver tray contained small packets of white powder. 'Would you like an 'up' sir?' he asked, smirking.

Rory stared coldly at the legalised pusher. Unlike the majority in the room he had always chosen not to partake.

'Up yours,' he replied, as he and Penny merged into the throng.

An hour was as much as Rory could take. He left Penny in the safe hands of two more of her friends, collected his coat and headed back out of the restaurant, just as the party was beginning to get more raucous.

The hard rain continued to streak down in torrents from the dark skies above the tall buildings that lined both sides of the street.

As Rory hurried on his way he risked a glance upwards, where cascades of water bounced off the roofs of the office and apartment blocks and sheeted through the auras created by the bright street lights.

'At least this weather proves there's one thing left The City can't control,' he thought as he strode along the glistening pavement, dodging the water that had formed puddles on the road and beside the kerbs. As he lowered his eyes back to street level he spotted a tremendously large man tanking along underneath an umbrella, firm in the belief that his sheer size would force everyone else to get out of his way.

Annoyingly, he was right.

'Evening, Rory,' boomed a voice from somewhere between the umbrella and the prominent stomach that almost broadsided the young journalist as he skipped to one side.

Rory recognised the voice almost as quickly as he recognised the man's monster girth. 'Evening, Doc – where are you...?'

'Can't stop young man – got to be somewhere – you know how it is!'

Rory thought he did know. 'Dr' Johnson's nocturnal trips were an open secret among his colleagues at the newspaper. The highly unlikely health correspondent of the City Daily was an inveterate cinemagoer who was known to be a fan of the black and white vintage B-movies of the mid-20th century, particularly science fiction and horror films.

Rory was quite sure that the good doctor was on his way to the Odyssey Picture House to get his weekly fix at the evening nostalgia screening.

As his colleague splashed his way down the street, waving a fleshy hand in farewell, Rory stepped back into the centre of the pavement to continue his journey home.

Here in the business district the streets were now relatively devoid of people. It would be very different, he knew, in the night-time quarter, which would be heaving no matter what the weather.

Having left the restaurant launch as soon as he politely could, and earlier turned down an invitation from colleagues to join the madding crowds for the evening, Rory was looking forward to getting home.

He enjoyed his job but still found it difficult to accept that, like everything else in The City, the Daily was ultimately answerable to the government so the amount of autonomy and freedom its journalists had was limited.

The Daily was the only official source of news, and those who worked for its broadcast and online teams were regarded as holding privileged positions of trust.

So, despite the restrictions he had to work under, being a news journalist was about as good a job as Rory could hope for.

He wasn't overly interested in the making of money for the sake of it and the idea of working in banking, accountancy or real estate – the roles that were seen as the most important and prestigious in this consumerist, financially fixated society – left him cold.

As such, he was an anomaly in The City, which was now run as a separate territory by its government which oversaw life within its borders as if it were truly a state of its own.

Following yet another major financial crisis, The Board had been appointed by the country's top civil servants to stop the constant cycle of boom and bust, and to put an end to the political short-termism that the previous adversarial democratic system had inevitably led to.

Faced also with major long-term challenges of how to deal with the environment, energy and public health, the people came to agree that a different system of government that enabled sustainable, long-term planning was needed.

The Board's business-like approach had proved so financially successful that The City now paid for the rest of the nation, which it administered at arms' length through a network of local government offices.

Those fortunate enough to be born Citizens worked hard and played hard, given every opportunity to make money and enjoy a vigorous, exciting life.

But they had to pay a price, for like so many of the products they constantly bought to keep the economy moving, they too were disposable.

In this great economic powerhouse in which workers' stars could shoot so high, those of the unwary would fall to earth very quickly, burnt out and soon forgotten.

Rory knew that many people found life on the downward slide overwhelming once the demands grew too much for them. Those who were no longer able to support the lifestyles they craved were not allowed to remain and become a drain on The City. They would be Removed and sent to live on the Outside once their period of economic usefulness had passed.

Rory was also aware of others who, unable to cope any longer, had committed suicide or opted to visit Terminus clinic to book a legal assisted death, rather than face the shame of their failure.

Money and greed were the cornerstones of this City. It was an insatiable, rapacious need for what was seen as success that had led the country's capital down this path, and it was this same need, now further entrenched by a fear of going backwards, that sustained it. It was an often cruel place where self-interest came first for most people, particularly the young.

But, Rory admitted, when things were going well you had little to complain about. The Board, wary that its unelected status should become a cause for resentment or opposition, strained every collective sinew to make sure that the Citizens had the most efficient services possible, while a constant public relations blitz reminded them how lucky they were every day.

Positive messages screamed from the massed ranks of electronic billboards that blighted every major commercial street, creating an unceasing, metallic cacophony of sound and vision shrieking empty promises into the ears of often empty heads.

Several such messages, mixed with adverts, competed for Rory's attention now as he turned the corner into another wet street.

'The City's Success is YOUR Success,' he read on one screen, while another proclaimed: 'The City Never Sleeps' before switching to a series of adverts for new apartments, for tickets to the next big sports matches that took place every evening – and for foreign holidays.

The latter were encouraged to approved, or green-listed, destinations that The Board had agreed deals with, via air travel either from the expanded City Airport or the monolithic Heathrow travel hub which now encompassed an ever-increasing area to the west, and to which fast transport links took you direct to any one of the seven terminals in minutes.

But right now, despite the weather, a trip abroad was the last thing on Rory's mind.

As he tried to close his ears to the slogans and promotions, he felt something swoosh low above his head and looked up to spot a police drone sweeping down from the sky.

Then he saw a man leap from the doorway of a shop halfway along the street, cannoning into a middle-aged couple who were walking past, before sprawling to the ground.

The man scrambled to his feet and ran.

The drone zeroed in and pursued him, a blue light flashing beneath it, capturing the scene as the runaway headed for what he hoped was safety. Rory thought he knew better. The fugitive had little prospect of escape.

Sure enough, he had barely reached the end of the street when two police vehicles came screeching into the road, one from each end, acting on the information being sent by the drone.

The driver of the first Snatch Squad car shot across his path to block his escape route.

The second SS car handbraked to a halt behind him, two occupants leaping from it to jump on the runner and quickly subdue and restrain him.

He'd had no chance and it was all over in seconds.

Rory watched from afar as the officers bundled the man into the car, setting off immediately in the direction of Central HQ, where Rory knew his identity would be checked against the criminal database. The journalist wondered what the unknown runaway had done and what fate awaited him.

Assuming his crime was relatively minor, what was found on the database would determine his punishment. If he had no previous record he may simply be banished from entering The City for a set period of time. Facial recognition cameras would almost certainly pick him up if he tried to flout the ban, and if he did, he'd be banned for life.

But if he was already known to the police, he would most likely be sent to one of the labour campuses on the Outside, where he would be put to work for several years producing the consumer products that City dwellers relied on to live their frantic, material lives.

Each of these campuses consisted of a series of factories, which had been set up to stop the country relying on increasingly costly imported goods from the Far East and other parts of the globe.

The campuses were major employers of people living further away from The City on the Outside, while some of the factories – the workhouses – were secure centres for anyone forcibly Removed from The City – Citizen or Outsider – for criminal or antisocial behaviour.

A life on the factory production line – that could be this man's most realistic hope for the future, until he was no longer deemed useful. After that, he would have no future, only a past.

Rory reached the shop the fugitive had run from.

The sign above the frosted windows read BBR. It stood for Blonde, Brunette, Redhead, and was a licensed sex shop. Here, you took your choice of any one of those options (others were available) to pay to spend time with. That was if you were a Citizen of course. None of the shops in The City were really for Outsiders, and certainly not this type of establishment.

It was obvious from the look of the fugitive that he wasn't from The City, so he would have been refused service. It was unlikely his identity card had even been requested before the police were notified, hence the drone and the speedy response from the Snatch Squad cars.

Rory knew one of their garrisons was just a few blocks away and it would have taken them no time, ready as they would have been to hit the streets at the first call for help, to arrive on the scene.

He shook his head.

Having no interest in sampling the colourful delights of BBR, he continued his journey home, eventually arriving at the doors of Templar Court, the building which housed the apartment he lived in.

Chapter 3

A DIFFERENT BREED

Rory entered the impressive steel and glass atrium and turned immediately to the lifts, one of which arrived within seconds. He got in and pressed the button for the 14th floor.

The glass cage rose swiftly and silently, and he found himself at his own front door almost before he realised it. Letting himself in, he switched on the light in the hallway, dropped his passkey onto the console table, took off his black brogues, hung up his sopping coat and headed for the bathroom.

After towelling dry his hair, he walked into the living room and across to the floor to ceiling window that formed one wall. The rain lashed against it with such vehemence that he inadvertently flinched – it was difficult to believe he was actually indoors.

He looked out across his corner of The City.

Almost opposite him, two blocks were being rebuilt so he could see further than he would usually be able to as they were both in the early stages of their race skywards. Beyond them he watched with childlike fascination as the High Line monorail train sped across the skyline, the shadows of its passengers showing dark against the lit-up windows.

He wondered where those Citizens were going at this time of

the day. Were they heading for the refuge of home as he had done or beginning another exciting but wearying night out?

Probably, some of the passengers would be Outsiders who, having finished their work providing the services Citizens took for granted, would be on their way to the major terminals to be ferried back beyond the City walls where life was so different from inside this careering juggernaut of a metropolis.

As he considered the lives of these unknown people, Rory's thoughts turned back to someone he had met just once, whose fate he had been discussing with Penny earlier that evening at the restaurant: Lorna Sexton.

Lorna was a clerk in the People Department, and she was not the sort of person you expected to disappear.

At 27 years of age, she was a good Citizen in every way, working hard in her civil service job four days a week and spending her three days of designated leisure time in the approved fashion – socialising, playing or watching sport, eating out, shopping or just chilling out at home in the electronic world.

She spent her state salary sensibly, covering her costs without resorting to borrowing, and was by all accounts a pleasant and intelligent woman as well as a diligent colleague.

What's more, she was loyal to, and therefore loved by, her friends.

Yet three weeks ago, Lorna Sexton hadn't turned up at work, she wasn't at her flat, her friends hadn't heard from her and her mobile phone number could not be contacted.

At the People Department, her tasks were reallocated, her desk and chair assigned to somebody else. The work keeping tabs on all Citizens carried on as usual without her.

So far, her flat remained empty but Rory knew that situation would not last for long. It would soon be let by the Estate Department to somebody else and all trace of Lorna would be eradicated.

It was unusual for someone so young and without any obvious stain on their character to be Removed like this – for Rory was sure she had been. The question was: why?

Lorna was hardly a drain on The City's resources – in fact, quite the opposite. She was, undeniably, an asset.

Which meant she must either have done something wildly out of character or discovered something she shouldn't have.

All in all, Rory thought the latter was more likely.

According to Penny, Lorna loved City life and enjoyed all it had to offer so the idea that she would have transgressed in any serious way, putting her future at risk, was fanciful.

And, he told himself, even in the unlikely event that she had, he would have found out as the City Justice Service was part of his beat at the Daily.

There were relatively few examples of Citizens, rather than Outsiders, being brought before the courts.

But when they were, The Board made sure the cases were publicised – the old-fashioned practice of justice being seen to be done was one of the big deterrents used to keep individuals in order. That, and the harsh penalties meted out.

Rory turned away from the window and checked the emails on his phone, finding, as he had expected, no positive replies from anyone he had asked about Lorna's whereabouts.

The more he thought about it the more convinced he became that the answer must lie within the People Department itself.

'People' was one of the most sensitive of the government departments to work for. Its main role was ensuring the number of taxpaying Citizens remained around the optimum level for the high standard of public services to be maintained affordably. Some felt this effectively gave the department power over life and death.

The subject was of such sensitivity to the government that any breaches of security would be a big issue.

Even with the media under its control, The Board remained keen not to allow anything to leak out that could risk The City's ostensibly happy equilibrium being upset.

Rory knew that his safest course of action was to go back to Penny and simply report that he had checked everywhere but could find no trace of her friend.

But he didn't think he could live with himself if he just left it at that. And after all, today... Lorna Sexton, tomorrow...?

Rory had many good contacts in government departments, built up over the years. But before calling in any favours he would need to be certain that whoever he approached would be helpful and that any questions would not lead to his own head being raised above the parapet, assuming it hadn't been already.

Unable to decide what to do for the best, he sat down and tried to clear his mind by going to the Daily's online 24-hour news channel.

He went straight to the top 10 most-read news stories of the day and scrolled down the list.

1. DeliverUp reveals most popular takeaways;
2. Tonight's football – live updates;
3. Reality star's online hate campaign.

Rory shook his head as he read further down the list.

'Drivel,' he muttered, as he saw the next stories concerned either the private lives of pampered sports stars or inane social media personalities plugging their latest shows.

At number 10, at the bottom of the list, he clicked on the link to the first serious story he found: a recorded government statement about the 25th anniversary of The City's breeding programme.

The screen showed a good-looking, dark-haired man aged around 30 standing at a podium and looking straight down the camera lens into the living rooms of those who could be bothered to watch.

Rory didn't need the on-screen caption to tell him that this was the slick and upwardly mobile Byron St John, a man he had seen across the room at the restaurant launch earlier and whose responsibilities included finding new ways of maintaining and improving The City's financial performance both now and in the future.

'BSJ' was tipped for great things; an already successful financier who was famous for his appetite for hard work and fast living. Those who knew him had told Rory he could be convivial company but that he was ruthless and thoroughly untrustworthy, even by City standards.

Rory was also aware, as was anyone who had watched him down the years, that he was a polished performer on screen.

With a smile, St John began speaking.

'My fellow Citizens, I am delighted to be talking to you tonight to mark the remarkable success, 25 years on, of The City's breeding programme. It seems almost incredible to believe that it was a quarter of a century ago today that The Board introduced this initiative, which has proved to be so successful in helping to secure a stable population down the years.

'As you know, this programme has relieved the majority of you of the worry, burden and expense of bringing up your own children, but enabled those who want it to have a paid-for career raising the young people our City needs in a fashion that makes them fully equipped for the challenges and requirements of modern life, ensuring they leave education ready to contribute to society immediately.'

St John's words made Rory think back to the little that he remembered of his own childhood, and of the guardians who had brought him up to learn the ways of The City. He thought of them fondly – both retired now – two people who had never hidden their view that not everything in The City was rosy and who had taught Rory, quietly and carefully, of the importance of thinking for himself.

They had been old enough to know what real parents were and they had tried to be that to Rory.

He missed them.

Back on the screen, the effusive Byron St John was now in full flow.

'So successful has this strategy proven in fact that, tonight, on the 25th anniversary of its inception – or perhaps I should say, con-ception,' he leered, 'I am able to reveal to you a new policy designed to build on its success and maintain our population at an affordable number in the years ahead.

'It will not only ensure we can continue to provide your public services to the high standard you deserve but, for the first time, will also offer a helping hand to those who feel their contribution to the life of The City may soon be coming to an end.

'From tonight, I am very pleased to announce, any Citizen who believes they might benefit from a slower pace of life will be able to apply voluntarily for early retirement and a resettlement grant which will help them to arrange their affairs and move to the Outside at a time of their own choosing.

'The grant will be given as a thank-you to them from the government for all their hard work and service to The City down the years.

'This generous grant will ensure they can move on their own terms and receive financial help to start a new life without facing the stigma of Removal.

'The City has invested in refurbishing attractive estates of homes in carefully selected seaside towns on the Outside which will offer an enjoyable and healthy way of life that will be ideally suited to former Citizens looking to move on to the next stage of their lives.

'Full details of how to apply for early retirement are now available on the government website...'

Rory was stunned – the idea that The City was now planning to contribute towards people's retirement rather than just throwing them out to fend for themselves was an unexpected about-turn and one he struggled to accept at face value.

He was watching St John complete his statement with an obviously plastic smile when the doorbell rang.

Without any premonition of what was about to overtake him, he stood up, crossed the room and went out into the hallway to open the door.

Two men dressed in the black uniforms of the City Police stood outside in the corridor. As he looked at them questioningly, one of them held up a phone to Rory's face, scanned it and nodded to his colleague.

It was the second man who spoke. 'We'd like you to come with us please, Mr Kennet.'

Rory hesitated, just for a moment.

'What's the problem?' he asked.

'We've just been asked to take you in to Central HQ, Mr Kennet. Would you come with us straight away – please?'

Despite the late addition of the polite interrogative, Rory knew it was a question in name only. He also knew it wasn't worth his time arguing.

With a growing sense of unease, he put back on his still wet brogues and coat, pocketed his passkey, turned off the light and closed the front door behind him on the way out.

As Rory descended in the lift with a police officer on either side of him and then emerged into the lobby of Templar Court, he had no idea that this was the last time he was to see the apartment he had called home for the previous two years.

Chapter 4

REMOVAL

Rory was driven to Central HQ, where he had his identity confirmed again with another scan at the front desk before he was taken through to a small, white-painted room.

Inside this room was a slim, neat-looking black man with closely cropped, grizzled grey hair, who stood up from behind a white desk that was placed in the centre of the floor.

He indicated a chair on the opposite side of the desk and invited Rory to sit down. The two officers who had come to his apartment were still with him and now ranged themselves on either side of his chair.

The neat man sat down again and turned briefly to a screen on the right-hand corner of the desk. He looked back towards Rory, before speaking in an unexpectedly deep, rich voice that was at odds with his appearance.

'May I see your identity card please, Mr Kennet?' he asked and held out his right hand.

The short car journey, during which both police officers had remained taciturn and uncommunicative, had deepened the feeling Rory had experienced as he had left Templar Court that all was far from well. He could not help but take a shallow breath before replying, as he took his City ID card from his wallet and handed it over, saying: 'May I ask why I have been brought here please?'

The man behind the desk kept hold of the ID card and replied quickly, with the competence and disinterest of the professional civil servant.

'It has come to our attention that you have been making inquiries into the People Department, which is of course outside your remit as a City Daily journalist. You will be aware, I am sure, Mr Kennet, that the workings of the People Department must remain completely confidential due to the necessity for data protection.'

He averted his hard, brown eyes for a moment, touched the screen and looked back at Rory.

'Journalists on the City Daily enjoy positions of great privilege, Mr Kennet. I am exceedingly sorry that you have chosen to abuse that position.

'It means you can no longer be trusted by The City.'

The uncompromising eyes remained on Rory's face and then the man reached down beside his desk and shredded Rory's ID card.

Rory stared across the table at him in disbelief. He opened his mouth to protest. 'You have got this completely wrong,' he said. 'I wasn't investigating the People Department.'

The man looked back at him and then turned to the police officer on Rory's left and said: 'Please take Mr Kennet away now.'

As Rory stood up angrily, his arms were gripped from each side and pulled roughly together behind his back. He felt the chill of cold metal touch both his wrists and heard the click of the handcuffs locking. At the same time the second policeman went through his pockets, removing his flat's passkey, his wallet and his phone.

Rory could do nothing as he was marched out of the room. The two officers led him along the corridor until, at its end, they stood at the top of a short flight of steps which led down to the basement of Central HQ. Rory knew, thanks to his job, that this was the Removes Area.

He was walked down the stairs and pushed forward into a white-washed brick cell measuring 8ft by 8ft.

Behind him, one of the silent agents deftly unlocked and removed the handcuffs.

As the door closed on him Rory looked at the low, slatted wooden bench attached to the wall of the cell and, his resistance for the moment exhausted, walked over and slumped down in a disbelieving heap, his back against the wall in more ways than one.

At 8am the next morning, the door was opened and in came two different officers, both of whom were over 6ft tall and seemed almost as wide.

'Time to go, Mr Kennet,' said the first as he hauled on Rory's left arm to bring him to his feet. As Rory got up from the bench, his hands were quickly manacled behind his back again.

He started to ask questions of the two men, only to find they became as silent as the pair he had dealt with the previous night so he gave up the one-sided conversation.

The three of them left the cell, went back up the shallow set of steps and out through the metal back door of Central HQ, which led onto a car park. Directly in front of them stood a large, unmarked car. It was painted black, and its rear and side windows were blacked out as well. It had an air of metallic menace. It was to this that the two police officers marched him.

One of them pushed him into the car through the right rear passenger door before getting in alongside him.

Rory remained silent. He knew there was nothing he could say to change the situation but his mind was still whirling at the way his life had been turned upside down within a matter of hours.

A couple of questions about a woman he hardly knew on behalf of a friend and his rights as a Citizen were to be taken from him, though he had led a blemish-free existence until that point.

What was it that the authorities thought he had discovered about the disappearance of Lorna Sexton? If they had simply been concerned that he was straying beyond his remit he might have expected a little downward pressure to drop his inquiries but that would surely be that – he couldn't believe for a moment that his innocuous queries had been worthy of a decision to Remove him.

The second police officer got into the front of the vehicle and Rory felt the car move beneath him as the bulky driver eased himself into his seat before starting the engine and setting his course.

Rory saw their destination show on the dashboard screen as the driver plotted it in: Workhouse A5.

So, he was headed for one of the secure workhouses where all his waking hours would be spent on a production line to help satisfy the voracious, never-ending consumer appetite of The City.

He knew roughly where Workhouse A5 was – off to the north-west, many miles into the Outside, and far enough away to be out of sight and out of mind to even those few in The City who knew of its existence.

A place with a gate that only opened in one direction.

The police car left the Central HQ car park and threaded its way through the busy streets, avoiding the hireable little Buzzers – individual, electrically-propelled pods that shot people around The City like tiny positive impulses through the body economic.

It picked up speed, following its remorseless path through the crowds of people going about their noisy day-to-day existence, just as Rory himself had done until the rainy evening that had brought to an end not only the day before but also the charmed life he had lived until now.

After rounding Marble Arch, the car was driven up Edgware Road, stopping briefly at one of the electronic checkpoints which granted entry and exit to vehicles coming into or leaving The City on the few major routes that remained officially open.

It headed into the suburbs, up the long straight Roman road that would eventually take it to Workhouse A5, driving through increasingly drab streets as the gilded City inside its financially continent electronic walls was left behind.

The streetscape became progressively grimmer as the outer extent of once comfortable suburbia was reached; shabby shops and empty, grimy buildings lining the long, unfolding road.

Then the countryside came into view through the one-way windows. Green fields shot past as the car entered what had once been the prosperous, self-satisfied shires – now known purely and simply to those to whom City life was everything, as the Outside.

Looking through the front windscreen of the car, over the driver's shoulder, Rory read a neglected road sign that welcomed him to St Albans and saw a hill looming ahead of them with a broad, majestic building at its summit.

Then there was a bang and Rory was flung to one side as the car veered across the road as if driven by an unleashed drunk on the binge of a lifetime.

It struck the kerb at speed, then was lifted into the air. Its chassis screeched across the top of a low stone wall and struck the rising parkland before flipping over onto its roof. Flames began to shoot from beneath its bonnet as the pyrotechnics began.

Chapter 5

THE PHOENIX RISES

Both the guards were unconscious, knocked out in the crash.

Rory was lying upside down in the car, his back against the inside of the roof. His body was hemmed in by the bulk of one of the policemen and, with his wrists still handcuffed, his arms were all but useless.

He writhed around, trying to create some space. He got his legs clear and started kicking against the inside of first the door and then the window in an increasingly frenzied attempt to get out.

He knew that this was his one chance to escape the living death that the workhouse would be. First, he had to avoid an unplanned cremation.

But his efforts failed to budge the door, which was stuck fast, and Rory could now see flames dancing outside the car windows. The secure cabin of the car was, for the moment, keeping the fire at bay but it was growing hotter inside by the second and Rory knew that he hadn't long left.

His kicks became feebler as the heat overwhelmed him. The door of the car and the orange of the flames were getting farther and farther away as his field of vision dwindled. Then, just as he was about to pass out, he heard the window smash.

Rory felt cooler air rush in as shards of glass scattered over him. He saw a thick arm thrust in from outside and felt a strong hand pulling hard at his jacket, helping to free him from the funereal embrace of his captor and to slide through the gap where the window had been.

He was bundled onto the grass before his unknown saviour started to run, dragging Rory behind him.

He felt himself bouncing along before he heard a thumping roar and the force of the explosion made his rescuer tumble to the ground.

Pieces of charred metal shot into the air and Rory was aware of a searing pain as a wave of heat struck his body and face.

That was as much as he remembered.

Gradually, noises, at first far-off, then suddenly closer, began to become clearer.

Rory breathed out; a shallow breath. His face felt strange; tight; as though something was pressing on the skin. He tried to open his eyes. He couldn't do it. He could imagine, rather than see, a deep, inky blackness all around him.

Panic gripped him for a moment and his right hand moved, tried to hold on to something... anything. His fingers found a metal rail and he wrapped them round it.

Rory realised he was lying down and tried to pull himself up but the flat palm of a strong hand pushed him gently back down again as a rough but kindly voice boomed out: 'Nurse... nurse! He's awake!'

Light footsteps came running, and he heard a quiet female voice. 'Please don't panic... you're in hospital... you have been involved in an accident. Try to stay calm.'

Memories were coming back to him now... his Removal, an accident, fire... and then that blessed moment of relief when he realised someone had got him out of the car that he had thought was about to become his tomb.

Rory moved his lips to try to speak, but even that slight movement hurt. He felt two hands manoeuvre him into a sitting position.

A glass of water was lifted to his lips and the soothing voice came again, repeating some of the words from before. 'You're safe; you're in hospital and we are taking good care of you.'

'How... how badly am I hurt?' Rory could barely recognise his own voice as he squeezed the words out through his parched throat.

The man's voice – the one that had called for the nurse – replied.

'I don't know how much you remember, but you were in a car accident and the car exploded.'

Rory did his best to nod. He managed some more words.

'I remember. Was it you who saved me – who got me out?'

The reply came immediately. 'Yes, that was me. Clarry's me name. What's yours? We couldn't find any ID on you.'

'My name's Rory – Rory Kennet.' He took a deeper breath. 'I'd like to shake your hand Clarry, but I don't think I can right now,' he managed to wave his bandaged right hand a little.

'Yes, well, there's no easy way to say this,' Clarry continued, waving away the protest that the nurse was about to make. 'You burned your hands and some of your face. So that's why you're covered in bandages, in case you was wonderin'.'

Despite a momentary feeling of horror as Clarry's words sank in, Rory tried a smile, though it didn't really work. 'Break it to me gently, won't you?' he said.

This time the nurse did get in first and shot Clarry a warning glance. 'I think that's quite enough for now, Mr Kennet. You need to get some rest and then the doctor will come and talk to you and discuss where we go from here. But your injuries have been very well treated – and you'll be fine.'

Rory nodded. But his brief show of personality had taken it out of him. His head sank back onto the pillows and within seconds he was asleep once again.

The next time he woke, he still couldn't see, but he thought there was a little more light in front of his eyes. The all-pervading darkness that had so frightened him when he first awoke appeared a little less, well, dark. This time he imagined he saw grey, not black.

Clarry's voice spoke from next to the bed he was still lying on.

'So you're with us again then? That's a good sign that is.'

Rory's skin still felt tight but his lips were working.

'Can you tell me what's happened to me?'

'I've been told to wait for the doctor.'

'Tell me anyway. When he comes, I'll pretend to be surprised. He won't be able to tell from my face anyhow.'

Clarry laughed, a sound that seemed to have travelled a long way from its starting point.

'All right, I'll tell you what I can. If I suddenly shut up it's because the nurse or the doctor's appeared, OK?'

'OK.'

'I saw what happened and went to help. After I got you out of the car, I got you to hospital. You've got some burns and normally, out here, you wouldn't have been able to get very good treatment for them.

'But the doctors kept you sedated while they managed to get some plastic surgeons from The City to come and work on you.

'There's an organisation some surgeons are part of, and they come here to the Outside and perform operations for free when they can because they don't agree that the best healthcare should only go to those that can afford it. It's called St something or other Society.'

'The St Raphael Society – it's named after the patron saint of healing,' said Rory. 'I've heard about it. I'd always thought it was a great idea.'

'Yes, well, you were lucky that the right people were available to come out,' said Clarry.

'Anyway, the other good news is that they reckon they have salvaged your good looks, though you might not look exactly the same as you did before, so they tell me.'

Rory sat back against the pillows. He thought about what Clarry had said and realised that he had got away lightly. He could have died in that car, or been horribly and permanently maimed, or faced the rest of his life in the workhouse.

'Not the worst outcome,' he said.

'No,' came another, authoritative male voice from somewhere to Rory's right. 'Not the worst outcome at all.'

The doctor, who said his name was Robert Sterling, gave Clarry a knowing look and stood next to Rory's bed, proceeding to tell him what he knew Clarry had already explained, albeit using slightly different words.

'You will need to stay here a few more weeks just so we can take off these bandages and then monitor you, but you should be as good as new – or perhaps better – and ready to fight another day. You've been fortunate, Mr Kennet.'

Rory lay back on his pillows. 'I don't disagree, doctor,' he said.

As Rory recovered, his bandages were taken off and he was able to see himself in the mirror for the first time.

He was, unsurprisingly, nervous that morning. But he was amazed at what he saw. The surgeons had done a remarkable job and, though he looked a little different, he was still himself, he was still Rory.

Now he was able to see again he felt able to discuss in more detail with Clarry the events that had brought him to the hospital.

'I thought you were a goner, mate, I really did,' said the man who Rory now knew to be called by the rather wonderful full name of Clarence Lionheart.

'No chance of getting them others out though. Sorry about that.'

'I can't pretend they were exactly friends of mine,' Rory said, and he told Clarry his story in full: about his job, how he had begun looking into Lorna Sexton's disappearance after being asked to by Penny and the shock of his own Removal.

Clarry said: 'Well, that explains the handcuffs anyway.'

Clarry was a phlegmatic barrel of a man. He was only of medium height but what he lacked in inches tall he made up with in inches broad. His chest was huge, his shoulders wide, his arms thick and tattooed with wrists as strong as iron. He was almost completely bald with just a few small strands of hair on the top of his head, and he had the lived-in face of someone who had boxed in his youth which, Rory judged, would have been somewhere around 30 years ago.

Clarry paid his way in life, Rory learnt, by running a fruit and veg stall at the market in St Albans town centre at the top of the hill where Rory's accident had taken place.

His voice was as booming as his back was broad and could be heard six days a week bawling out his offers on everything from caulis to cabbages from halfway down the road.

Everyone knew Clarry. He was, in the argot, a bit of a local legend.

He explained that he had been on his way back to his stall after picking up some produce from a nearby farm when he had seen the car taking Rory to Workhouse A5 make its unscheduled diversion.

He waved away Rory's expression of gratitude with a bluffness that endeared him to the journalist because he could see in the big man's eyes that it actually meant a lot to him.

Then Clarry sighed and said: 'O'course, you do know it were no accident, don't you?'

Rory looked at him. 'What makes you say that?' he asked.

'Well, everything happened so fast, but I know what I saw. There was a small explosion under the car that forced it off the road. The explosion caused the crash – not the other way round. And I don't see how that could have been accidental.'

Rory thought swiftly. 'That's interesting,' he said.

'Because that would mean I was never intended to reach the workhouse. It also means that those two policemen were expendable. Anyone blowing up that car could never have expected any of us to survive.'

Clarry agreed. 'Thinking about it, I reckon the only reason you weren't killed outright was because the bomb didn't go off properly before the crash.

'But The City won't know that as there wasn't much left of that car after the second explosion.'

Rory nodded. 'I think you're right. The police will have sent someone out to check on it – all their cars are tracked on every journey they make – but the chances of them being able to identify any remains there may be among that heap of ash are pretty low. And that could be rather good news for me,' he added thoughtfully.

Clarry laughed, a sound that rumbled from deep within his cask of a chest.

'Yep – I reckon you're in the clear all right. But it does leave you with a problem. The City thinks you're dead, so you can't go back there as they'd arrest you again as soon as look at you. Which means you're going to have to get used to the way of life out here. I've never lived in The City, obviously, but I'm pretty sure living on the Outside is a bit different to what you've been used to.'

'Different, maybe, but rather more real I suspect,' said Rory.

'I'm not bothered about not going back to The City. To be honest with you, Clarry, I've always thought there was a lot wrong with it. But that doesn't mean I'm done with the place yet. I want to find out why they Removed me and tried to murder me over something so innocuous – and what happened to Lorna Sexton too.'

Clarry snorted. 'Well, you can count on me to help you in any way I can. I love what you're sayin', although you might only be sayin' it because of that knock on the 'ead you had. You oughta be dead really, but instead you've risen like that bird, that's what you've done, like that bird.'

Rory looked quizzical and then he smiled, and his eyes widened.

'I know what you're talking about, Clarry. Like the Phoenix from the ashes, is what you mean. Like the Phoenix from the ashes.'

Chapter 6

ON THE OUTSIDE

When Rory was fit to leave hospital, Clarry insisted he stay with him, his wife Ruth and their daughter Lily.

Their home was a former pub that many years ago had been converted into a three bedroomed house. For some reason Rory couldn't fathom it was painted bright yellow, but the years had, from that point of view, been kind to it, dulling its primrose tint to something rather easier on the eye.

The Lionhearts' yellow house was home to Rory Kennet for three months and the genuine warmth of their hospitality never wavered for a single day.

For the first few days, Rory didn't leave the building, as he sought both mentally and physically to rebuild from the enormous, life-changing jolt he had received.

Then, as he began to feel better, he set out on walks in and around the town to see things for himself.

Clarry went with him a few times early on, partly to keep an eye on him (he felt sure Rory wasn't as recovered from the crash and surgery as he claimed to be) and partly to vouch for him and introduce him to people. He also didn't want his new friend's early experiences of meeting more Outsiders to be bad ones.

In truth, many of the people Rory met in his first few weeks of venturing out helped to restore his faith in humanity. Although some of them were, he had to admit, a little on the rough and ready side compared to the slick plasticity of most City dwellers, he saw in their eyes and felt in their handshakes a blunt honesty that he respected.

Not once did he find himself being appraised slyly in the way so many Citizens would do whenever they met somebody new. Not a single time did he feel these people mentally calculating his net worth or whether he would have something they could use as they climbed up the greasy pole of society, politics and business.

So, as the days went by, Rory relaxed and so did Clarry. Rory's walks began to get longer, taking him beyond the town centre and out into the countryside, down little roads and even littler lanes, discovering tiny hamlets of houses, some occupied, some empty – each with walls that had borne blind witness to the antics, good and bad, of generation after generation.

For most of those years, these buildings had been home to families that continued, decade after decade, to enjoy an improving quality of life: higher incomes, more possessions – in theory, more happiness.

Now that had changed. Money and the incessant, squealing drive of The City and its devotees dominated everything, and the Outside played a weary second fiddle – at least in material terms.

This didn't bother Rory. As he settled into his new life, he was already finding a peace of mind that he had never experienced before; an inner contentedness that, until now, he had not even recognised was missing.

One crisp spring morning, after chatting with Clarry and his nephew Dickie, who helped his uncle run his fruit and veg stall, Rory went for one of his walks.

Along a side street he reached a set of moss-covered steps leading downwards. Taking care not to slip, Rory descended the first flight and found himself in a narrow alleyway lined on one side by shrubs and on the other by a brick wall of some vintage which gave off the unassuming scent of the suburbs.

A second flight of steps led from the alley to a set of garages. Built to house residents' cars in more prosperous days, they were now used to store all manner of goods that enterprising locals could get hold of to sell on for profit.

Rory looked around at the pull-up doors of the garages, many of which were disfigured with graffiti.

'Fuck The City' was just one of the witticisms he read.

Walking past the garages, Rory eventually emerged on to Lower Dagnall Street, from where he could see green fields in the distance.

He made his way down the road which was lined with a mix of Georgian, Victorian and late 20th century houses on each side, standing like sentries guarding access to the countryside ahead.

The cries of the market traders had receded into the distance and Rory was enjoying the quiet of what was still, though run-down, a pleasant residential area.

He had almost reached a crossroads when that peace was

broken by the urgent sound of people shouting.

He walked quickly towards the junction, turning left at the corner. As he entered the street he spotted two boys in hoodies running off in the opposite direction and then saw smoke streaming from the broken window of a cottage halfway along the terrace.

As he ran towards the scene of the fire, neighbours were coming out of their own homes, some screaming in panic as they saw the smoke.

Rory headed straight towards the house that was ablaze. A thin woman with lank, black hair stood outside, watching the drama unfold with one hand held in front of her mouth. Grabbing her arm, he asked: 'Is there anyone inside?'

The woman whipped round and Rory saw that her pinched face was marked with tears.

'Yes, my neighbour and her two kids were in there – I haven't seen them, I don't think they've got out yet,' she said urgently.

Rory didn't hesitate – adrenalin kicked in and he replied: 'I'll try to get them out – stay here!'

The smoke was now pouring from the broken ground floor window. As he sized up how best to get in, he heard an old man's voice shout from behind him: 'Wait for the fire brigade – you can't go in there, you'll be killed!'

But Rory kicked open the front door and found himself in a living room which was well ablaze. The smoke was thick here but he could see well enough to be sure that the room was empty of people. Then he heard a woman's voice shouting from above him. 'Up here! Help!'

In the corner of the living room was a staircase leading to the two bedrooms and bathroom that formed the first floor of the old workman's cottage.

Rory leapt up the stairs, reaching the fourth step in one effort and running up the remainder of the staircase. At the top, on the tiny landing, was a short, fair-haired woman whose plump and reddened face was frantic with worry.

'My two children are in the back bedroom! Can we get them out?' she cried.

He did his best to offer a reassuring smile though his mind was working out what their options were as he felt the heat of the fire begin to reach up the stairs behind him.

'We'll find a way,' he said with more confidence than he felt, and followed her into the back room where two scared-looking children aged six and seven years old were crying and hugging each other on one of the two single beds that took up most of the room's floorspace.

Rory shut the door and leapt on to the second of the beds which was pushed up against the wall, just as he felt the smoke he had been inhaling since he entered the house begin to have an effect on him.

It reminded him that he was hardly that fit yet. As his breathing became shallow he stood on the bed, willing himself to overcome the wave of tiredness that was engulfing his body.

He pushed up the sash window in the wall above the child's divan and began to feel better as the cool, clear air rushed into the blue-painted room.

He looked out of the window at the courtyard garden below

where he saw two men, one standing on either side of the 5ft high wooden fence on its right-hand side, manoeuvring a long wooden ladder.

'Up here – quickly,' he shouted to them.

Within seconds they had positioned the ladder against the side of the house and Rory helped first one child, then the other, out through the window before one of the men guided them down safely. Rory then insisted that their mother follow them.

Finally, it was his turn. Taking a deep breath of the clearer air outside, Rory threw his left leg over the window sill and felt for a rung of the ladder with his foot.

Another wave of tiredness struck him and, inexplicably, he missed his footing and found himself hanging onto the side of the ladder which moved beneath his weight as the two men below battled to keep it upright.

Rory's body swayed to and fro, before he crashed into the ladder, forcing the air from his lungs. But he managed to fasten his right hand to the other side, halting his momentum.

At the same time, he became aware that his acrobatics had been viewed by several other people as he heard a collective gasp rise from the courtyard beneath him.

After taking a moment to collect himself he tentatively lowered his left, then his right, foot down a rung on the ladder before he felt two strong hands grip his calves from below and help him, swiftly but carefully, down the remaining steps.

As he gratefully rediscovered terra firma, Rory turned to find anxious but smiling faces staring at him and heard voices congratulating and thanking him. Then he heard one voice he recognised booming above all the others: 'There'll be time for all that later – let's get away from the house!'

There, on the edge of the crowd that had gathered in the garden, was the unmistakeable Clarence Lionheart, who had seen the smoke and heard the commotion and descended from the market along with half a dozen of his fellow traders.

'Come on Rory, for Gawd's sake let's get away from here,' shouted Clarry as he bulldozed his way through the little group of thankful well-wishers, and clapped the two ladder-bearers on the back with a huge hand which was intended to convey his approval but nearly knocked them both over.

Rory permitted himself to be almost bear-hugged through the crowd.

'You only left me five minutes ago – can't you try to keep yerself out of trouble for more than that? And what is it about you and fires – you can't stay away from 'em!' grumbled Clarry as the group of rescuers, rescued and onlookers reached the end of the small, terraced row, pushed their way down a side alley and back out onto the road, where yet more neighbours had gathered from surrounding streets.

Rory's grime-blackened face erupted into a huge grin.

'You're right, it does seem to be becoming a bit of an issue, doesn't it?' he said.

Clarry grunted, as the sounds of a siren could be heard above the noise of the crowd. 'Not sure it's a larfin' matter meself, Rory, but well done on what you just did there – you're a proper hero.'

As Rory shivered, Clarry took off his thick, black wool jacket and wound it round the younger man. 'Come on home with me for a while, let's get you into the warm and get some food inside you, there's no point waitin' around here – let the professionals do their bit.'

'Just one thing Clarry – what about the family from the house – where will they go?' asked Rory.

From behind him, a woman's voice rang out. 'Don't you worry, they can stay with us while all this is sorted out. And thank you for what you did.'

Rory turned to see the thin woman he had first encountered when he had arrived, but Clarry grabbed hold of his left shoulder and propelled him round as a fire engine entered the street.

'That's right – we look after our own round here,' he said. 'Now, come on hero, let's get you home before you catch your death of cold,' and he marched him off back up the hill.

Clarry looked at his friend, who was still shivering in spite of the coat wrapped around him.

'Most people run away from danger, not towards it – particularly when that danger is a blazing house. You're a brave man, Rory, and no doubt about it,' he said.

Chapter 7

THE STATION

Rory was keen to not presume too much upon the goodwill of Clarry and Ruth, even though they showed no signs of wanting him to move out. But he knew he had to find somewhere of his own to live – and to work out a means of supporting himself.

He found walking the best way to think things through properly; it had the added benefit of helping him to get to know the town and the neighbouring countryside.

A week after his rescue of the mother and her two young children from the blazing cottage, Rory headed out east of the town centre. It was a pleasantly warm, if largely overcast, day and he had just passed a housing estate on the fringes of the town when he came upon a small, wooded area.

The wood was cut off from the winding lane by a low iron fence that had originally been painted dark green. Now the paint was chipped off in most places, revealing brown, rusted metal.

Rory walked along the length of the fence until he spotted a stile which let him into the wood. He found himself on a track which was overgrown and appeared little used and was soon striding punchily along. He left the wood behind, passing through a patch of scrubland. After 10 minutes his left foot kicked against something, causing him to stumble.

Instinctively, he put out his right hand to save himself and touched a metal rail. Beneath it he discovered a thick wooden sleeper and realised that he had come across an old railway line which was obscured by the thick undergrowth.

Rory followed the line, interested to find out if it went anywhere or, as he expected it to, petered out.

He saw ahead of him on his left-hand side a concrete platform. As he reached it, he could see that it had once been part of a station or, more accurately, a halt. The platform, which was covered in moss and grass, was empty other than two iron posts which would once have held a sign with the station's name.

Still curious to see where the track headed, Rory continued to follow it, in places having to push his way through a mass of weeds that had grown up around the line over the years.

Another mile farther on, he saw a short tunnel cutting through earthworks that rose on each side and he headed towards it. As he entered the tunnel, he felt the temperature drop noticeably as the gloom enclosed him. But he could see light just a few hundred yards ahead and he had an overwhelming, if completely irrational, feeling that the tunnel was a gateway to somewhere good, instead of being the dingy, underground road to nowhere it appeared to be.

When he reached the end of the tunnel, Rory saw another platform in front of him, this time part of a bigger station than the halt he had just left behind. A single-storey station building remained intact, standing several feet back from the track itself. Beyond it, farther along the single rail line, stood a signal box.

He climbed the slope of the platform and walked towards the building. A wooden canopy held up by wrought iron stanchions protected the red-bricked front of the Victorian building from the elements and what would have been the worst of the smoke from the trains in the distant past.

The doors and window frames, like the canopy, had all previously been painted in either green or cream, though they were now in a tatty, sorry state. Rory walked up to the main doors. Though they were still locked, they were partly rotten, and he pushed his way, with little effort, into what had been the main booking hall.

He looked around. The cream paint was peeling off the walls of the long, oblong room, but its high ceilings and multiple windows meant it maintained a light and spacious feel even though the grime on those of the glass panes that remained in place filtered the strongest of the sun's rays.

He walked to the left where a door gave into a room that had once been the ticket office, and he smiled as he examined the period features that remained, including the tattered remnants of posters that had invited travellers to visit seaside resorts, and the station signage.

Then he explored the remainder of the building, discovering what had been waiting rooms, toilets and an office and rest room that he presumed the railway staff must have used.

He left by the main doors and walked towards the platform's edge, where a white painted strip could still be seen. He stood, hands on his hips, gazing across the track. Opposite were a handful of sheds in a siding, fed by a spur that led off the main line, on which stood a train carriage and goods wagon that looked like restoration projects.

Beyond them was a grass bank – a natural phenomenon that was replicated behind the station building, so the station sat within what was effectively a private cutting, one entrance to which was the tunnel Rory had approached through.

He looked towards the dilapidated but still graceful signal box on his left and made his way along the platform and down the slope towards it.

As he approached, he gazed down the line, noting that it disappeared round a bend beyond the edge of the cutting.

The signal box was unlocked. He pushed open the door which was beneath a set of wooden steps that led up to the first floor.

Walking round inside, he saw there was enough space to create two good sized rooms. In one corner was a solid internal staircase which he climbed, emerging into the single room that ran the length of the first floor and had once contained the signalling equipment.

This was flooded with natural light by deep windows on three sides which offered clear views of both approaches to the station as well as beyond the grass bank opposite.

Rory took a deep breath as he surveyed the lie of the land in front of him, enjoying the feeling of peace that had enveloped him. 'This is it,' he thought. 'This is going to be my home.'

Back at the yellow house on the hill that evening, Rory raised his discovery of the station with Clarry and Ruth over dinner.

Clarry said: 'I knew there was an old railway line there Rory, but I didn't think there'd be anything much left of any of the station buildings, I must admit.'

'The thing is Clarry, would you have any idea who owns it? You see, I'd rather like to buy it,' said Rory.

'Buy it? Whatever for? And what with?' asked Clarry, in disbelief.

Rory laughed. 'To live in. But I don't know quite how I'll be able to raise the money – yet.'

Clarry looked at Ruth. 'Told you 'is 'ead still wasn't right.'

Ruth shook her own head at her husband. 'Don't be so rude, Clarry. Are you going to help Rory or not?'

'Course I am,' replied the grocer, gruffly. 'Only kiddin' wasn't I?'

His eyes smiled as he looked across the table at Rory. 'You won't need to buy it though. Nobody owns those railway lines – they were closed even before The City as we know it now came about and all the companies that used to run the trains and owned the land don't exist anymore. I reckon you just go in and take it over.

'Though I imagine it's going to take a bit of work to turn it into a home that someone from The City would be happy with. Luckily for you, I happen to know a lot of people who'd be able to help.

'As for paying them, I'll sort that for you – you can pay me back later on when you get yerself sorted out.'

A delighted Rory could scarcely believe the generosity that Clarry showed towards him, and he vowed there and then to find the quickest possible way to pay him back.

Over the next few months, Rory enlisted the help of many of Clarry's friends and tradespeople contacts as he set about the not inconsiderable task of renovating and furnishing the old station building and the signal box. Amongst those he met first was a young man named Exeter Pikey.

Petty crime was all Exe had known. His name marked him out as a loser. Born in unfashionable Devon and with an unknown traveller for a father, he had left the West Country as a teenager after his mother had died but was never thought likely to amount for anything hanging around the fringes of the great, shining City.

However, refusing to accept his lot, he embraced the challenges life had thrown at him and determined his own course to attain success.

His sharp wits, dark good looks and innate bravery had stood him in good stead and his career, such as it was, had many high points, most of which included daring raids into The City, followed by exhilarating chases and escapes that had made his name legendary – and hugely popular – among the community of Outsiders, especially as he was wise enough not to target his neighbours and was happy to share the spoils of his successes with those in need.

But when he was not venturing inside the electronic walls to carry out burglaries, Exe was also a dab hand at painting and decorating. Hence, he was among the many contacts from Clarry's address book who proved to be just what Rory required for the physical work of renovating the old station.

He and Rory quickly became firm friends and allies. And, like

Clarry, Exe knew a lot of very useful people.

As he considered how best to fund both himself and his planned investigation into The City's Removals policy, Rory had swiftly decided to take Exe into his confidence.

He told the thief one morning: 'One thing I'm going to need is full access to the internet – and another is a security system for this place.'

On the Outside, the internet was restricted by The Board, so sites that could be viewed included mainly entertainment, shopping (for those who had money) and unlimited pornography.

There was one official news site but as everyone knew it was rigorously controlled by The City, very few took it seriously. There were no discussion forums and no facility for questioning or criticism. Any unapproved sites that were put up were swiftly blocked before being taken down.

But Rory knew that the internet inside The City was very different, and he was determined to access it to keep up to date with what was going on. So, finding someone who could help him do this without being discovered was imperative.

Rory was having this discussion while perched on the third rung of a tall step ladder looking up at Exe, who was standing on top of it with a roller in his hand, turning light grey plaster into a smart ceiling.

'I know exactly who you need,' said Exe. 'Jolly Roger.'

Risking a drop or two of white paint in his eyes, Rory replied: 'I have a feeling I'm going to regret asking you this, but who the hell is Jolly Roger?'

Exe chuckled at his own joke (he knew it was coming).

'Well, that's not really his name but he is a bit of a modern-day pirate when it comes to the internet. He's a techy whizz and he's just who you need to speak to. Trust me on this one,' he said, turning his face back up towards the job in hand, 'Jolly Roger's your man.'

For the first time of many, Rory found he had no reason to doubt Exe.

Jolly Roger (Rory was a little disappointed to discover his real name was actually just Roger Jolly) did indeed turn out to be all Exe said he was.

What Roger didn't know about electronics and programming wasn't worth knowing and, had he been born in The City, he would have had a stellar career.

Completely self-taught, and utterly obsessive, he was a bean-pole of a man, in his mid-20s and with long black hair that fell to his shoulders that he was continually having to shift away from his face with either or both of his hands. When you could see his face, he had a long thin nose, thin lips and blue eyes of a striking intensity. He spoke in a similar vein, rapping out his words quickly as if keen to get the conversation over and move on to something far more interesting.

He and Rory, with Exe listening in, had several detailed discussions about just what Rory wanted and how it could be achieved.

Roger set about installing a series of security measures in and around the station, impressing Rory with both his theory and practice, suggesting little refinements here and there that showed him to be imaginative and thoughtful as well as technically brilliant. When it came to Rory's worries about overcoming the internet restrictions, he was almost scornful.

'Course it can be done – it's easy. What's not so easy is stopping them spotting you after a while. We'll have to keep updating things, but I can do that,' he insisted. 'Leave it to me. I'll sort it for you.'

While Roger was doing exactly as he promised, Exe was introducing Rory to another of his friends with expertise in a different area that was to be put to an imaginative use by Rory, whose emotions at his enforced Removal from The City, while not overtly obvious to anyone else, had grown to include not only anger but also a desire for justice that bordered on retribution.

'This is Stella,' said Exe, simply, indicating a tall, slim, woman in her early 20s who stood at his side.

'Stella,' he continued, 'is the chemist you wanted.'

'Stella who?' enquired Rory as he appraised the newcomer's thin face and shoulder-length ash blonde hair, thinking she looked more like the product of a City school than a likely associate of Exe's.

'Just Stella,' she answered, in a firm, quiet voice.

'That's all you need to know. So, what is it exactly you're looking for from me?'

After being momentarily taken aback by her directness, Rory couldn't stop a smile breaking out on his face.

'Follow me, and we'll talk about it,' he said, leading the way down the platform and across the railway line, which was now free of weeds, to the sheds on the opposite side of the track, one of which had been converted into a workshop.

He looked at Exe, who smiled back at him and nodded, before adding: 'Then I'll tell you exactly what I'm thinking.'

Within three months, Rory and his team of workers had turned the old station and its signal box annexe into a very comfortable and highly secure home.

Rory had also found a handful of lieutenants he knew he would be able to rely on to help him in their very different ways, and a wider group of friends he could call on in a crisis.

While the work had been carried out, Rory had been thinking long and hard about what he should do next. As his sense of injustice over what had happened to him grew, he became even more determined to find out the reasons behind both his own Removal and that of Lorna Sexton.

His experiences so far of the Outside and, more specifically, the people he had met there, had put another idea into his head: the setting-up of a fund to help deserving Outsiders, particularly those he felt had been dealt a poor hand by The City. He explained to a delighted Clarry and Exe that he had decided to call this The Phoenix Fund.

Rory had also become less squeamish about how to raise the money he needed. The more he thought about how he had been treated, the less worried he became about not playing by the rules.

Inspired by Exe's tales of the many successful raids he had made into The City, Rory decided the most fitting way to raise the money he wanted was to redistribute some from certain people there who, he felt, had rather more than they strictly required.

To help him, Rory knew that Exe would be the ideal ally.

Rory was aware that many rich Citizens avoided taxes by keeping some of their wealth on currency cards which, once cash had been allocated to them, were untraceable. This not only made theft from them possible but also meant it was unlikely that they would report their losses.

So, Rory and Exe discussed and planned a series of raids on likely specimens that Exe then successfully carried out over the next two months.

It proved to be a perfect partnership, with Rory's knowledge of The City and some of its more dubious but very rich characters combining with Exe's renowned skill set of audacious burglary followed by turbo-charged escape.

As Exe showed his brilliance, Rory's fund grew by the week.

He now planned one glorious final theft – with a twist – which, if it could be pulled off, should not only yield another financial windfall but would also strike at the very heart of The City's political powerbase.

Chapter 8

ASHES TO ASHES

Exe looked over his shoulder as he ran for his life down the narrow, dimly lit street.

His burglary of Byron St John's home having been successfully accomplished, he now faced his biggest challenge – getting away safely.

He knew that what The City would regard as his pointless existence hung by a thread. If the drones found him and alerted a Snatch Squad his career of thieving, and now arson, would almost certainly be at an end.

Exe ran around a corner and spotted a gap between two houses on his right-hand side. He felt sure he could outwit the drones if he could just reach the alleyway before they entered the street, so he ran as even he had never run before, his lungs bursting with the extra effort until he made it to the dark passageway.

Here, just outside The City in what remained of the innermost of the old suburbs, the streets were drab and largely empty. Bit by bit, the buildings were in the process of being demolished and their occupants forced to move because of The Clearance.

The Clearance was creating an open ring of land between The City and the Outside, making it easier to monitor the major roads which remained open and restrict entry and exit to those and the approved trains and rapid transit systems.

The area, so near to and yet so far away from the immaculate City, was a mess, and this alleyway was dark, dank and filled with rubbish. But it was rubbish that was useful to Exe right at that moment, and he dived beneath an old pine table that was partially covered by a filthy piece of carpet.

Doing his best to ignore the dismally damp smell, he pulled the carpet down further over the sides of the table so that it blanked out the feeble light that showed from the single streetlamp that still worked, and waited, trying hard to control his breathing and slow his fast-beating heart.

The drones were all but silent, so he had no way of knowing whether they had passed on down the street or continued to hover around the area, meaning his only safe strategy was to stay put for some time, hoping they would be recalled or sent to another incident.

He lay as still as possible for nearly an hour before finally stretching his long legs and easing himself out from beneath the rickety table and its fetid Axminster.

The air was clear; the drones were nowhere to be seen and he checked that the currency cards he had stolen were still inside his black jacket.

Knowing their loss would not have been discovered because he had covered up the theft by committing arson, he made his way to the spot where he had hidden his car.

Once the favoured form of transport throughout the world, private vehicles had long been superseded inside The City itself by the now ubiquitous Buzzers.

But Exe loved his. He started it up and enjoyed the full-throated roar of the engine, marvelling once again at its ability to start first time after all these years.

Of course, he did look after it, regularly taking part in the races on the abandoned small airfield on the Outside, where his prowess was widely acknowledged. Here, the boy racers would gather and burn through petrol like mad demons.

Exe stamped his foot down on the accelerator pedal as the powerful headlamps carved out a route for him on the wide road ahead. He quickly reached Watford before road conditions forced him to reduce his speed.

Driving more slowly now, he passed through several roundabouts, weeds growing all over them, before forking left at Leavesden just before a stone monument.

It must have been erected for a reason. Now it just stood there, in between two stretches of road on a small area of sad, unkempt grassland, about 15ft high, weather-beaten and with three words spray-painted on it in white 4ft high capital letters – PITY THE CITY.

The words, which Exe's headlights had picked out as he took the left fork, has been there for years but were evidently repainted regularly by somebody as they appeared clear and bright again whenever the ravages of the weather threatened to dull the paint. Exe had no idea who did it or why.

He turned onto a dual carriageway on which the road markings were becoming ever more degraded, speeding up again as he headed onto the last leg of his journey towards home. Passing a now little-used motorway junction, he looked up into the night sky where he could see the light twinkling on top of the cathedral on the hill that dominated the area and could be seen for miles around during daylight hours, like a giant beacon of hope overlooking a sea of resignation.

Five minutes later he was at the top of the hill, and he turned left down the forlorn High Street lined by grand old buildings that had once been at the heart of a thriving town centre.

Now they retained just a faded grandeur, continuing to service a much poorer population whose consumer requirements, compared with those of the Citizens, were like their expectations for the future – pitifully small.

Exe drove past the dreary frontages of shops where the mainly hand-painted signs were mostly in need of refresh and repair, though the occasional one looked well looked after – their shopkeepers ever hopeful that those who made an effort would entice more customers.

The noisy car drove past the cathedral, through the Abbey Gateway, a great flint archway that had stood for nearly 700 years, and into the narrow Abbey Mill Lane. On the left was the still beautiful Verulamium Park with its lakes, Roman remains and acres of grassland, though they were now invisible in the darkness.

Exe pulled up outside a small row of cottages. Just one streetlamp showed a timid light and even Exe, who knew this area well, felt a slight shiver down his spine as he got out of the car, locked it and looked to the left and right before pushing open the low iron gate, striding up the short path and leaping the two steps to the age-dulled, red-painted front door.

He turned the key and entered his four-roomed home.

He switched on a light and closed the thick curtains at the single front window. In one corner of the room, he moved a wooden cabinet slightly to one side. After opening its door, he felt inside and withdrew a slim screwdriver which he used to unscrew both ends of a floorboard.

From within the cavity, he took out a lacquered black box which he unlocked using a tiny key from his keyring and placed the cards he had stolen earlier from Byron St John's home inside before locking the box, replacing the floorboard and screwdriver and moving the cabinet back to its original position.

Ten minutes later, the cottage shook as the soles of heavy boots met the area around the lock of Exe's front door. The latch gave way and two 6ft-plus intruders in the black uniforms of City Police pushed their way into the living room.

'Down – now – get on the floor!'

It was an instruction, not an invitation, and one that Exeter Pikey obeyed with alacrity. He hadn't survived as long as he had done without knowing when the odds were so stacked against him that to argue was futile.

On the dusty wooden floorboards he lay, face down, as the first of the two officers stepped further into the room and stood over him, quickly but efficiently running his black-gloved hands through Exe's clothing. Then he pulled him to his feet by the back of his jacket, whirled him round and almost threw him onto the sofa that backed against the left-hand wall of the room.

'You set fire to a property in The City tonight – tell us why now – it's your only chance to save yourself!' he shouted.

His voice brooked no disagreement and nor did the gun which he aimed at Exe's head.

Exeter Pikey saw death looking him in the face and felt cold beads of sweat emerge under his dark hair and drip down his forehead.

Whatever else people might say about him, Exe was no idiot. He had just opened his mouth to speak when, from the front doorway, a new voice spoke quietly but with undisguised authority.

'Officer, I have you covered. Put the gun down on the floor now and both of you take a step backwards and turn around. Do it please, and do it now,' the fourth man commanded, with a remarkable politeness bearing in mind the gravity of the situation.

The two policemen were used to taking orders but not from disembodied voices in strange little cottages on the Outside and both took their eyes from the thin man on the sofa as they turned to face the speaker.

Which was exactly what Rory Kennet had expected to happen. As the first officer with the gun wheeled round, Rory kicked at his wrist, dislodging the weapon which pirouetted through the air before falling helpfully into Rory's own left hand.

The look of dismay mixed with anger on the police officer's face was comical to see but the gun that Rory now held stopped both him and his colleague from doing anything rash.

They looked at the hold-up man, who stood nonchalantly in

the doorway, leaning against the frame.

He was not overly tall, standing at around 5ft 9ins, but he was slim and lithe and athletic looking, which made him seem taller, as did his well-fitting navy suit. His striking face had character, with prominent cheekbones and a strong chin, though the skin seemed strangely stretched on one side.

A lazy smile played on his thinnish lips which did not match the look of bleak hostility in the grey-blue eyes that were set perhaps a little too wide apart underneath a shock of dark hair.

His voice was gentle and quiet and was somehow even more effective for it.

'And next, I think we'll have the time-honoured tradition of hands in the air where I can see them, whilst my friend here makes sure you have no more damaging pieces of kit on you.'

Exe had breathed a sigh of relief deeply but silently when his rescuer had first spoken and had leapt up from the sofa without having to be asked. He frisked the two officers, enjoying the neat and swift reversal of roles, and took another gun from the second man, as well as two pairs of handcuffs and their keys.

'Hang on to that gun, will you?' asked Rory, who, though unused to firearms, was now holding court and rather enjoying himself.

The first police officer stared at the man who now held all the aces as well as his automatic. He was not without courage himself and ventured a comment: 'Whoever you are, you won't get away with this.'

He gestured backwards towards Exe. 'This man entered The City this evening and set fire to the house of a prominent

Citizen. If we don't take him in, others will come to find out why not. You should walk away now and let us do our job. Then at least you may be able to escape the justice that is due to you both for a little while longer.'

The man in the doorway smiled once more. 'I'm afraid that simply won't happen.'

He also gestured towards Exe. 'This man, as you put it, was doing a job for me tonight and, as usual, he seems to have done it rather well, so I won't be leaving him to what you call justice. I know all too well what that would mean for him.'

Despite Rory's languid smile the words he then spoke were far from lazy as he turned towards Exe. 'Secure these two, will you? They'll have to remain here for a while as we make ourselves scarce.'

Exe used the two pairs of handcuffs he had taken from the officers to manacle them both.

Rory said to him quietly: 'I'm afraid you'll have to move home for a bit too.'

'Didn't you know I'm an itinerant? The clue's in the name you know,' whispered back the whippet-like Exe.

Turning back to the police officers, he said: 'After you,' before forcing them one in front of the other up the stairs that led from the corner of the room to the first floor of the cottage.

Exe had used the front bedroom to sleep in but the smaller back room was empty, with bare walls, an unvarnished wooden floor and a single unshaded lightbulb hanging from the ceiling.

Having switched on the light to see the two prisoners in, he kept his gun on them as he forced them into a corner of the room.

He felt above the door frame and took down a small length of thin but strong rope which lay along the top of it – one of several precautions he had taken in case of need. He used it to secure the two men via their handcuffs to the wall-mounted radiator which sat beneath the window, after which he returned to the doorway and flicked off the light again.

He looked at the men who would have either taken him in or ended his life just a matter of minutes ago.

'You should think yourselves lucky,' he told them. 'Your colleagues will probably come and find you soon enough when you don't report in. You'll live to fight another day.'

He added, almost as an afterthought: 'You should be pretty relieved he let you go.'

The second officer spoke up for the first time. 'He doesn't look, or speak, like a killer.'

Exeter Pikey stared at him. 'That what you reckon is it? You keep telling yourself that,' and he left the room, closed the door and locked it with a brass key which he then took out and pocketed.

He shouted down the stairs. 'Have I got time to pack?'

'If you're quick,' came the calm voice from below. 'And I mean quick, there are bound to be more of them here soon.'

'Quick is my middle name,' lied Exe as he entered his own room. He walked to the wardrobe and took out a battered but still beautiful leather holdall he had acquired on one of his missions and started filling it with clothes.

Task accomplished, the light traveller descended the stairs and rejoined his rescuer in the living room of the cottage that had been his home for the past six months.

'Do you have the cards on you?' asked Rory.

'What do you take me for? They were already hidden when those two arrived,' replied Exe and promptly went to the cabinet in the corner of the room and repeated his earlier manoeuvres, this time taking the stolen currency cards from the small lacquered box.

Rory grinned. 'I always have faith in you, Exe. Come on, it's time we got out of here. I think you'd better come and stop with me for the time being. Regrettably, I fear this lovely little spot will be too hot for you for a while.'

They left the cottage and walked down the short path to the street which ran alongside the park. 'Do you mind if we take your car?' asked Rory. 'Mine's parked up the road, we can come back for it another time.'

Exe had started up the engine when they both noticed a set of headlamps coming down the hill from the historic gateway at pace towards them. There was no noise from the black electric vehicle that they recognised as another City Police car.

Rory was about to speak but Exe was away down the road before a word could leave his mouth. The police vehicle followed as the driver spotted them leaving and the two cars headed down the hill alongside the darkened park at an increasing speed.

It was not destined to be a long chase. Exe had the advantage of knowing that the road was a dead end, leading to one of England's oldest pubs, Ye Olde Fighting Cocks, at the corner of the park so as he neared the building he switched off his headlamps and slid the car into a small parking area on the right-hand side of the street, ready to head back up the road.

The police car drove on straight ahead and the driver had little time to react as the iron railings that marked the end of the road and the beginning of the park loomed up in his lights. He avoided a head-on collision, but the car still struck the kerb, before hitting the railings side on and ploughing through them into the undergrowth.

Rory got out of Exe's car and ran over to the scene of the crash. Seeing that the two occupants had managed to free themselves and were wearily pulling themselves away from the wreckage, he took a small round object, stamped with an illustration of a bird rising from the ashes, from his jacket pocket, took careful aim and threw it into the abandoned police car.

'With the compliments of The Phoenix,' he called out to the two dazed officers whose faces were suddenly lit up by the blaze caused as the little firebomb created by 'Just Stella' exploded.

Ten minutes later, Exe's car came to a standstill behind the single-storey station building which stood on the platform on the other side of a low white picket fence. Both men got out from the car, Exe grabbing his treasured leather holdall with what remained of his worldly goods, while Rory led the way towards a gate in the fence that sat to the right of the weather-beaten red-brick building.

Rory opened the green-painted wooden door of the Station House and invited Exe in, waving him to a homely fabric-covered armchair by a large fireplace. He himself sat down on a small, stylish sofa covered in moquette fabric that had been one of his favourite finds in an antiques shop when he was furnishing the house.

Exe flopped down and said: 'You know, I thought I'd finally had it when they sent the bloody drones after me again. I've never run so fast! And I can still smell a piece of mouldy old carpet I had to hide under for what felt like hours to escape them. I guess a drone must have spotted me when I left the suburbs – I can't think how those police would have got on to me otherwise.'

'You're probably right. But as I told you before – I have great faith in you,' Rory smiled again. 'Did you get all you expected to?'

Exe took the box of cards from inside his jacket. 'You bet. I guess this little lot will keep us going for quite some time.'

Rory nodded. 'Well, it's certainly going to help. Let's get it transferred,' and he pulled a small device from his pocket on which he tapped each of the cards one at a time.

He smiled as he checked his account a moment later.

'All done,' he said. 'I think we have enough now to cover almost any eventuality – and to launch The Phoenix Fund.'

Exe threw him a glance. 'That's going to make you a very popular man, you know,' he said.

'It's going to make me a very helpful man, Exe. I just want any deserving person in difficult circumstances to know they can get a little help from time to time if they need it. And I want to give something back to say thank-you for the way I've been helped since I came here. That's all.

'I've decided on my first person to help as well.'

'Oh yes?' said Exe. 'Who's it to be?'

'The woman I rescued from the burning cottage a few months back. I checked and it seems two boys I spotted running away had firebombed the place for kicks and she and her children are still relying on their neighbours as they don't have the money to pay for repairs. So I'm going to sort that out for her.'

'That's a great idea Rory, you'll be making a real difference there.'

Exe stretched out his long legs on the thick rug in front of the fireplace before failing to stifle a yawn. 'Sorry,' he said.

Rory was not offended. 'Look, it's been a long night. Let's get you up to the signal box – I take it you're happy to doss down there for a while?'

Exe smiled at the idea that living in the signal box was 'dossing down'. Having been one of those who helped to transform it, he knew that it spared little on luxury.

'I think I can manage that, if you're sure you don't mind putting me up for a bit,' he said.

'It's the least I can do. You can stay as long as you want to.'

Exe picked up his holdall while Rory led the way out of the Station House, along the platform, down the slope and by the side of the railway track.

In front of them lay the signal box, which they could now see much better as the security lighting came on. A set of renovated wooden steps with a banister on the outside led directly up to the first floor living area with its deep windows that offered a fabulous view over the surrounding woods and countryside and, as Rory had been quick to appreciate, also acted as an ideal lookout post.

Beneath the steps was the door which led to the ground floor, which now contained a kitchen, bathroom and bedroom in this upside-down home, leaving the panoramic views from the first floor to be fully appreciated during the daytime from the large living area.

Rory quite often took himself up there to make the most of the complete sense of tranquillity it offered.

As a result, he knew just how special a place it was and was sure that Exe, and anyone else who might need it in the future, would be happy and comfortable there.

He handed Exe a key. 'You know your way around and the bed is already made up. I'll see you in the morning.'

The now visibly tired young man took the key with a grateful nod. Shrugging his bag from his shoulder into his right hand, he lazily raised the left to say good night.

Chapter 9

BARNABY EDGELEY

The next day, after a late breakfast with Exe, Rory headed up to the market to see Clarry.

It was just after midday on Wednesday and the market was beginning to wind down. Towns on the Outside had reverted to a custom last practised across the nation several decades earlier, which meant most shops closed for a half day once a week. The day varied between Tuesday and Thursday from area to area. Here, half day closing day was Wednesday.

Standing next to the stall, Rory updated his friend on the events of the previous night and the discussion soon turned to his planned investigation into The City's Removals policy.

'I'm still convinced the key to this lies in the People Department, Clarry. It's where Lorna worked and her disappearance effectively led to my own Removal. I need to find a way of getting a lead to the department if I'm to find out what lies behind all this,' said Rory.

The grocer replied: 'I've been thinkin' about it too and I reckon you could make a start with the government office here. There are representatives of the People Department there.'

'Are there?' Rory was surprised.

'Yep. There's a whole team responsible for approving – or taking away – the work permits for everyone who goes into The City every day. To do all those lovely, dirty jobs they don't want to do themselves,' he added contemptuously.

'And it just so happens that you're in luck, Mr Phoenix. Y'know my daughter Lily – well, she applied a couple of weeks ago for a permit and they're sending a man round to interview her at home on Friday. They always do that when you make your first application, to make sure you're a fit and proper person to grace the concrete.

'Why don't you come and see him for yourself? He's due to meet Lily at three o'clock. He's told her he has an important appointment with a City official afterwards and that her meeting will take about half an hour. Come for lunch at one.'

Rory considered the idea and nodded his head. 'Deal,' he said. 'I might enlist some help and see what this important appointment is about after he leaves you as well. You never know what you might find out that could prove useful later.'

'Right,' said Clarry. 'Well, Exe is your best man for that job, as you probably already guessed.'

Then he laughed as Rory was forced to move swiftly to one side. A determined bargain-hunter who had been standing a few feet away carefully watching the stall elbowed her way past him to get to the last remaining strawberries which Clarry was just marking down in price and had been about to shout about.

Lily Lionheart was a skinny lass of 19 who was looking forward to going to work in The City to start earning some money. She sat rather nervously through lunch with her parents and Rory, who she already knew well following his explosive introduction to the family, waiting for the clock to tick towards the scheduled time of her interview.

Lunch over, they all settled down to wait for the knock on the door which, when it came, led to Rory quietly moving into the little snug that opened off the main living room, a relic from the house's previous days as a pub. He knelt to look through the large keyhole in the door to see who he would later be following.

There was nothing particularly impressive about the man, who introduced himself as Barnaby Edgeley. He was of medium height, had brown hair, was clean-shaven and looked to be in his late 30s. His hair was ordinary, his clothes were ordinary – an off the peg suit that appeared smart enough when you first looked at it; he carried both a briefcase and a separate slim leather portfolio that were also ordinary – not too smart, not too shabby. In fact, he looked just like what he was – a nondescript civil servant.

Rory listened in to a routine interview in which Edgeley asked Lily several questions about her background, her aspirations and her work experience.

At the end of it, he said: 'Well, based on what you have told me I am happy to grant you a work permit. You will be sent a code which will give you access to an online database of available roles in The City which you can then apply for.

'After you have been accepted for your first post, you will be given a green card which will enable you to enter The City to carry out your work and leave at the end of each day. You can use it on either the trains or the electric rapid transit buses. I wish you luck with your search and hope you enjoy working in The City.'

Having dispensed this good news, Edgeley placed the tablet he had used to record Lily's details back in his briefcase, snapped it shut and picked up his separate portfolio which had remained untouched throughout.

He then stood up, shook hands with a thrilled and red-faced Lily and shouted a goodbye to Clarry and Ruth who had been listening without pretending very hard not to from the kitchen, before leaving through the front door.

From the side door that led to the cosy snug, Rory slipped out quietly, leaving the door ajar for Clarry to close after him as they had earlier agreed.

He watched Edgeley head up the hill towards the town centre and spied, on the other side of the road some 20 yards ahead of their quarry, Exeter Pikey in position.

Following at a discreet enough distance, he walked in the footsteps of the man from the People Department.

Barnaby Edgeley gave no indication that he had spotted the presence of either Rory or Exe. He simply continued up the hill into the town, turned left in the direction of the cathedral and, before he reached that great monument to a God-fearing past, slipped down a narrow covered alleyway that housed an arcade of small, cheap shops.

Here, the crowds were thicker, so Rory and Exe were careful to keep a close eye on their quarry. He walked on, passing a café at the end of the arcade before emerging onto a terrace bordered by the walled Vintry Garden on one side and a handful of mature trees on the other. The area backed on to the cathedral.

Just past the café, Edgeley opened the latch of a brown-painted wooden gate, passed though it and swiftly mounted the steps of a spiral, iron staircase. At the top of this was a door on which he knocked before stepping inside.

Rory indicated a table outside the café, looking onto the pleasant aspect of the cathedral, and Exe came over to join him.

They sat down and ordered coffee from a very young waitress who was beside them in seconds.

Rory looked up towards the office above the café where Barnaby Edgeley had gone. He saw the civil servant's head appear in the window. He was talking to another man, presumably, thought Rory, the City official he had mentioned to Lily.

Rory turned to Exe. 'Know of any other way out of there?' he asked.

Exe shook his head. 'There's none. That staircase is the only way. The only windows and doors are the ones you can see from here. Trust me, neither of them is going anywhere without us spotting them.'

The coffees arrived.

Exe emptied half of his large cup in one gulp and sat back in his wicker chair to listen to Rory explain all about Lily's meeting with Edgeley.

'So, what do you think he's doing up there, Rory? There's no way that's an official office of The City, that's for sure,' ventured Exe.

'No,' agreed Rory, 'and that's precisely why it's interesting. It seems fair to assume that whatever this office is for, it's got nothing to do with formal City business.'

Just as Rory finished speaking, they saw the door to the office open and Edgeley came out and descended the spiral staircase at a slightly more careful pace than he had gone up it, before closing the wooden gate behind him.

Exe said: 'Shall I follow him?'

Rory thought not. 'I wouldn't bother. Remember he had both a briefcase and a portfolio on him when we trailed him here? Well, he hasn't got the portfolio with him now, so if he had anything of any interest on him, I suspect it is now up there in that office.'

So they stayed where they were and ordered another coffee each. Twenty minutes later, they were rewarded for their patience.

This time they heard, rather than saw, the door to the office being closed and looked up as the man Barnaby Edgeley had been meeting with came down the stairs and out through the gate onto the terrace where they sat nursing their drinks.

'Well, well, well,' remarked Exe after the man had walked past them, oblivious to their scrutiny.

Rory arched an eyebrow. 'Don't tell me you know him?'

'Not by name, but I've seen him before. He was at Byron St John's mansion when I burgled it. I saw him with my own eyes talking to St John.

'Actually, they were thick as thieves themselves.'

Chapter 10

THE EXE FACTOR

Darkness had fallen on the shopping arcade at the back of the cathedral. The relative warmth of the day was already a memory and a strengthening wind was blowing through the trees. It buffeted the lichen-spotted wall of the Vintry Garden before spreading across the open parkland beyond.

Rory stood hidden amongst the line of trees which gave a good view of the footpath that lay between the garden and the grounds of the cathedral. When he was certain that no-one was coming along the path, he used the light on his phone to flash a signal in the direction of the closed café.

From a crouching position, a tall, lithe shape unfolded itself and moved across to the gate which led to the spiral staircase and the office to which Barnaby Edgeley had reported.

Having opened the gate, Exeter Pikey went quickly up the iron steps to the entrance of the office. He waited at the top to make sure there was no-one about.

While he had faith that Rory would warn him of any impending danger, long experience had taught him that taking every possible precaution was always the wisest move in his job, and he knew that Rory, promising though he was, was still learning the breaking and entering game. The only noise remained that of the wind, which seemed to be growing stronger with every passing minute, so much so that he heard a tree creak.

He effected his entry with the minimum of fuss and the maximum of skill, securing the door behind him in case it banged in the wind.

He checked that the blind was properly drawn at the window in the first room of the two-roomed office, only switching on a torch when he was certain no light could be seen from outside.

He wasted no time in going over the rooms. There was one desk in the first office and another in the second; the latter also featured a desktop computer, a filing cabinet, a second chair and a side table on which sat a kettle and some mugs next to a small sink.

Exe checked the drawers of the desk in the first room; other than a few pieces of paper and some stationery, there was nothing there.

The second room was a different story. Here, the drawers of the desk were locked, though not for long, as was the filing cabinet (ditto). Neither was a match for Exe.

He found Edgeley's leather portfolio locked inside a drawer of the filing cabinet. After carefully unzipping it, he went through all the documents within, photographing every one of them before relocking everything he had violated, leaving the filing cabinet and portfolio as he had found them.

He was determined that Byron St John's friend should notice nothing amiss the next day.

His work complete, Exe left the connecting door between the

offices open as it had been, locked the main door as he went out and again halted and checked that all was clear as he stood on the platform at the top of the steps.

He reached the courtyard at the bottom quickly before leaving through the gate and doing up the latch.

He joined Rory under the trees and nodded that all was well. The two of them walked swiftly along the path that led round one side of the cathedral to the graveyard that housed the remains of the locality's former great and good and still commemorated their lives; their existence otherwise forgotten.

Rory shivered inadvertently, drawing up his coat collar as the wind blew more strongly still; stirring up a swirl of dead leaves, bits of paper and other detritus left behind by earlier visitors.

They reached Rory's car, which he had parked in front of the cathedral.

'Get anything?' Rory asked.

Exe grinned. 'Everything, Rory, don't worry. If there was anything in there that will help us, we have it now.'

They both got into the car and circled Romeland Garden, waking the only one of the four vagrants making a bed of the wooden benches there who wasn't so drunk he was dead to the world, before heading out through the town centre.

Back at the Station House Rory and Exe sat in front of a screen looking through the images of the documents that Exe had found in the office.

They soon worked out that the name of the man Edgeley had been meeting there was Richard Brown.

At first there didn't appear to be anything else of obvious importance. But then they came across a short list of addresses.

There were just a dozen, all in areas that even Outsiders would have described as 'unpromising'.

Underneath these places were dates and times, together with notes. As they read down the list of addresses, all of which were within a few miles of the immediate area, Exe spotted one that caught his eye.

'Rory – look here,' he said, pointing to one line.

The address was preceded by the name Gower's Clock Shop and followed by a set of initials – BSJ – and a date of a week ago.

Those initials were indelibly etched on Exe's mind. They stood for the name of the politician and businessman whose home he had burgled just a few days earlier – the home where he had first set eyes on the man he now knew to be called Richard Brown.

But the address where he had once again proved the efficacy of his breaking and entering skills that night had been in one of the most exclusive streets in The City.

The address listed next to the initials of the one and only Byron St John this time was a very different one. Exe knew the road and district well. Seedy, down at heel and firmly on the Outside, it was most definitely not the sort of place one associated with The City's Deputy Finance Director.

'Interesting,' murmured Rory. 'Why on earth would Byron St John be meeting anyone out here?'

'And at an address like that?' asked Exe, in wonder.

'Rory, I know that place; it's an absolute pit – I wouldn't want to spend too much time there myself, never mind expect a man like St John to be seen dead there.'

Rory considered this for a moment. 'Yes, that is very strange.'

He looked back at the list in front of him with renewed interest. 'Have you seen this second line beneath it?'

Exe checked and saw that it was the next day's date, followed by the word 'Delivery' and a time, 8pm.

'I think I may take a trip to Mr Gower's emporium tomorrow evening and find out what's being delivered,' said Rory.

Exe replied: 'If you're going, so am I. I'm not saying you need a bodyguard, but I am telling you that you're going to have one.'

Rory smiled. 'That's fine. If the area's all you say it is, I might actually be glad of one.'

Chapter 11

RESCUE ON A DARKENED STREET

It was a funny colour of day. The heavy grey clouds seemed lower than Rory remembered ever seeing them before and were tinged with purple.

He stood motionless in the recessed doorway of an empty shop as the darkness descended with every passing minute. All along this once busy street the iron streetlamp columns stood rusting, their bulbs long extinguished and never replaced.

Feeling the onset of pins and needles, he stretched his left leg, then his right one, rarely taking his eyes from the untidy frontage of the tall building opposite.

This was the unlikely address associated with the name of Byron St John. Its ground floor was home to Gower's, a tired-looking shop where antique clocks were sold and repaired that only opened for a few hours on a handful of odd days every week and was now closed in this early evening. The two floors above looked to Rory as though they were probably used as flats.

A once white, now grey, net curtain stopped anyone outside seeing in through the rickety sash window of the room on the first floor, but the top floor window was curtainless.

However, it was barred with what looked like two iron stakes that descended from the lintel.

Rory looked at his watch. It was just before 8pm. He'd been here, standing in the doorway of the boarded-up former electrical shop, for almost two hours. It felt longer.

His eyes strayed along the road. Though he couldn't see him, he knew Exe was similarly hidden in the doorway of another shop. Farther along the street stood a grey car in which sat, seemingly asleep, the actually very alert Clarence Lionheart.

Rory was hopeful that a careful reconnaissance of the property today would pay off. He felt that the linking of St John's name to the address had to be significant.

And if anyone came to make this 'delivery' at 8pm, he had no doubt he would see them. They would use the front door – in this part of town there was no need to be careful about who saw you.

As Rory leaned against the peeling, grey-painted wall of the doorway, he looked again at his watch. The hands had moved round to 8pm.

He stretched and turned his eyes back to the faded, once elegant, frontage of the clock shop. Then he heard a noise from the direction of the end of the street.

A vehicle rounded the corner.

With no other traffic anywhere around, he was instantly alert. And as he watched, his eyes widened. He knew this kind of car.

It was all black, with blacked out windows. Just like the one that had taken him from the City Police Central HQ to the Outside where a piece of good fortune, aided by the strong arm of Clarry, had given him the chance of life anew.

In the ever-fading light, he watched the car pull up outside the clock shop.

As it halted, a City Police officer opened the front passenger door and got out.

After closing his door, he opened the rear one and stood in the centre of the empty road, ignoring a dented tin can that rattled past his right foot as a sudden gust of wind blew it along the Tarmac.

From within the car, a slim, dark-haired woman of about 5ft 4ins emerged. Her face, though perhaps not classically beautiful, was striking, with high cheekbones.

However, there was no denying that, right now, a scared look scarred her features.

It was the sort of face that would have stopped Rory Kennet in his tracks at any normal time. On this occasion it did more than that. For this was Penny Neave.

Rory was stunned. Penny – here – clearly in the hands of Removal officers, just as he himself had been all those months ago. Penny was the 'delivery'.

He had to make a split-second decision now – to intervene or to wait it out and see what happened next.

The brief he had given the others was to watch the address and see who came and went, to see if this would shed any light on its use and a possible link to Byron St John.

At a signal from him, either Exe or Clarry were ready to follow on foot or in the car anyone Rory deemed of interest.

While Rory watched, a second officer emerged from the other side of the car, making three of them including the driver, who appeared to be taking no interest in proceedings and remained sat behind the wheel.

'One more than they had for me,' Rory noted, wryly.

The two who had got out now stood one each side of Penny, walking her round behind the boot of the car before heading towards the door of the clock shop.

Rory made up his mind. He would allow the guards to take Penny into the building and continue the watching brief. He guessed she was in little imminent danger and was content to wait a bit longer before deciding what to do next.

As the two men and their captive approached the shop door it opened inwards; someone had been keeping an eye out for the car to arrive.

The door closed quickly behind the trio, giving Rory no chance of getting a glimpse of whoever had opened it.

He sidled out of his doorway, his dark clothes merging with the gloom, and made his way along the street to where he knew Exe was stationed.

Spotting his thin face, he motioned for Exe to follow him and the pair of them headed along the street to the car in which Clarry was waiting patiently.

Rory and Exe got in. Exe, who had a nose for anything unusual, was quick off the mark with his question.

'Who is she then?'

Rory smiled that knowing little half smile of his. 'You don't miss much, do you?' he asked back.

'Believe it or not, that is Penny Neave – I think you'll both have heard me mention her.'

Both Clarry, roused from his pretend slumber, and Exe showed genuine surprise.

'Penny? Blimey, Rory, what's that all about then?' was Clarry's reply, while Exe gave a short, quiet whistle through his teeth in response.

Rory said: 'It looks to me as though she's taking the trip I was treated to myself not so long ago.'

The other two looked at each other, questioningly. It was Exe who spoke first.

'I take it we're going to do something about that?'

Rory flashed a challenge to them both with eyes that could change from stone cold to warm and engaging in a matter of seconds.

'What do you think?' he asked, the flinty grey-blue giving way to a healthy glint of amusement.

Ten minutes later, Rory, Exe and Clarry were ready to put their quickly constructed plan into action. Clarry, being easily the biggest and most physical of the trio, his extra years notwithstanding, took the opening role. He walked round the block and approached the unmarked police car from the other end of the street, having spotted the driver get out, clearly bored, and light up a cigarette while leaning on the front wing.

Clarry had changed his gait markedly. Shuffling and wheezing, he came level with the driver, who had raised his eyes questioningly at his approach before lowering them again as he saw the man lumbering along.

Clarry then made his opening, if unoriginal, gambit.

'Gotta light, mate?' he asked, putting his left hand into the pocket of his bottle-green duffle coat.

'Sure.' The driver put his own hand into a pocket, seeking his lighter.

He was off his guard and soon off his feet too, after Clarry's right fist connected with his jaw. His left arm snaked round the falling driver's back to catch his fall, avoiding the thump his body might make if it were to strike the side of the car.

The big man had boxed rather well into the years beyond his youth, and he hadn't lost much of his strength, even if quicker feet than his would have taken him apart in the ring now. The driver was out for the count with the single punch and Clarry took the keys from the car ignition, opened the boot and bundled his unconscious victim into it.

His job done, he settled down into the driver's seat to await further developments.

At the rear of the property which housed the clock shop, two figures scaled the chest-high stone wall and took their time to carefully navigate the square courtyard, which was filled with pieces of discarded furniture, a rusting bicycle and two very full metal dustbins brimming with rubbish.

There was a rattling sound from the back door of the shop premises and a tiny, under-nourished old man – Gower himself – emerged with a plastic bag in his hand. Rory and Exe could just make him out in the shaft of light that escaped through the open door.

They watched from only a few yards away, backs against the

courtyard wall, as the old man lifted the lid of one of the dust-bins, saw there was no room in it and used his left hand to shove down on the rubbish inside.

He swore under his breath as his bony hand tore through a plastic bag that was on the top. He pulled out the hand and wiped two fingers on his trousers before adding the bag he had brought with him to the bin and pushing down the lid as hard as he could, until it was almost flush. Muttering in annoyance, he turned back towards the building, closing the door after him but making no attempt to secure it.

Rory and Exe looked at each other and both grinned. Exe moved first. He turned the handle and pushed open the door, finding himself in a corridor that led towards the front of the building and the one room used as the shop itself. Rory followed, after closing the door in the manner of the horologist before him.

Halfway along the corridor was a staircase that rose to the upper floors, and, beyond it, a room with a door that stood slightly ajar. Moving silently, Exe reached the doorway and peered in, watching as the old man sat down in a well-worn, wing-backed leather chair with his back to him, a TV screen flickering away on the wall opposite.

Over his ears were clamped a large pair of headphones that would almost certainly stop him hearing whatever went on in the rooms above him. Probably deliberately, thought Rory, who was at Exe's shoulder. Either way, he was going to be little trouble.

Rory looked at Exe, who nodded his head and pointed above.

The two of them went up the stairs, still taking care to avoid making any noise. They reached a landing on the first floor, pausing to take in the lie of the land. There were two doors, both of which were open. The one to the left was the door of the room at the front directly over the shop, the one with grubby net curtains overlooking the dusty street. It was empty. The door on the right opened into a bathroom. Again, no-one was in it.

It meant the two police officers were upstairs with Penny, thought Rory. It would be a two against two battle and he and Exe would have the very definite advantage of surprise.

He turned round to his confederate who smiled; he had had the same thought.

'Ready then, Rory?' Exe asked, quietly.

'When you are,' came the reply. Rory's face was set but excitement glittered in his eyes as Exe led the way up.

They reached the top floor where just one door faced them. It was closed. Rory kneeled at the keyhole, gratefully reflecting on the advantages of older buildings.

Inside, Penny was seated facing him on a wooden chair but not restrained in any way. The chair was in front of the barred window that Rory had earlier spotted from the doorway opposite. To her right, standing at a fireplace and with one arm resting on the mantelpiece above it, stood one of the two officers. The other was sat opposite him, on the edge of a single mattress on an iron bedstead. He didn't look particularly comfortable there.

The man by the fireplace, who was the one who had got out of the car first, was speaking, making no effort to keep his voice down, meaning Rory and Exe could hear every word without straining. He was answering a question Penny had put to him.

'You'll be kept here while we wait for someone to come to interview you again and give you one last chance to talk.

'This is what we call a holding house; it's under the control of The City authorities, obviously. You'll be interviewed later and will stay here tonight regardless. Tomorrow, assuming you have continued to be unhelpful, you will be taken to your final destination. Until then, we'll make you as comfortable as possible, but you may as well get used to a more spartan way of life, considering where you're headed.'

Penny's green eyes flashed at the man. Rory could tell she was scared but he admired the defiance in the gaze she shot at her captor. 'And where's that then?' she asked. 'Surely it doesn't have to remain a state secret now that I've been Removed? I mean, who am I going to tell?'

The second man spoke up from his odd berth. 'I would have thought you could work that out for yourself after all the information you've been busy gathering. While you're thinking about it, take time to consider that you'd still be enjoying your old life if you hadn't been so bloody nosy.'

Penny's eyes narrowed as she pursed her lips. Knowing she had little to lose gave her the added courage to reply as she wished.

'All I ever did was try to find out what had happened to a friend. I don't see how that's cause for anyone to be Removed. So if you call that kind of life something to enjoy then that's fine. I'm not quite so sure myself. I suspect there's a better way than The City does things. '

The first man took his elbow from the mantelpiece above the

fireplace and yawned theatrically.

He wasn't tired, just rude.

'Think what you like; say what you like. You're here now and tomorrow you'll be somewhere else where you won't be bothering anyone who matters with your thoughts. Anyone who wants to listen to you will be welcome to – if they've got time.'

He signalled to his colleague on the bed. 'C'mon, let's go downstairs and eat.' To Penny, he said: 'We'll bring you something up in a while, when we're done.'

He turned away from her and made his way towards the door. The other man rose from his uncomfortable-looking sitting position to follow him.

But, as the first officer strode out of the room after opening the door, he was tripped by the left leg of Rory Kennet and had his head smashed against the floor by Exeter Pikey, ending his active participation in events.

The second man was so astonished by what had just happened that he was caught completely on the back foot.

Exe leapt over the prostrate form of the first police officer and grabbed hold of the second man's throat with both hands, forcing him back across the room where a stunned Penny had jumped up from her chair as Rory followed Exe into the room.

'Rory?' she mouthed almost silently in disbelief as she recognised the man she had never expected to see again.

As the policeman tried to prise Exe's hands from his throat, the thief removed his right and gave him a quick, efficient jab in the stomach.

Winded and doubled up, the police officer was incapacitated

for long enough for Exe to snatch the man's own handcuffs from his belt, shackle his hands behind his back and shove him onto the low single bed.

Rory grabbed Penny by the hand and rushed out of the room. He and Exe then lifted the body of the first officer back inside before Rory shot home the two bolts on the outside of the door.

'Exe, meet Penny; Penny, meet Exe,' he said, performing introductions on the crowded landing as if they were all standing in the drawing room of a country manor house.

The three of them made their way quickly down the two flights of stairs. Once in the corridor on the ground floor, Rory pushed wide open the door of the room behind the shop.

Taking the headphones off the startled shopkeeper's ears as he began to turn around, Rory said: 'Time's up old man – your days of collaboration are behind you.

'This is your one chance to get away from here – I'd head out the back way if I were you,' and pointed the way out through the doorway.

Gower looked up fearfully at the grim look on Rory's face. 'Who the hell are you?' he croaked.

Rory couldn't help himself.

'You can tell your friends that The Phoenix has risen from the ashes,' he said, and seeing confusion in the old man's gaze, he reiterated the message. 'Don't forget – tell them about The Phoenix!'

The clockmaker scuttled away as quickly as he could, past the laughing Exe and the still disbelieving Penny.

Rory headed in the opposite direction and pushed aside

a heavy, dusty red curtain to enter the back of the shop. He motioned for Penny and Exe to go past him into the room of clocks and as they left through the front door he waited behind for a moment.

Clarry got out of the police car that stood outside as he saw Exe and Penny leave the shop, ready to head down the road to where his own car was waiting.

Before he joined them, Rory took a small round object, stamped with an illustration of a bird rising from the ashes, from his pocket, rolled it gently across the floor of the shop and banged the door shut.

They heard the explosion as they ran off down the darkened street.

Chapter 12

PENNY

Rory sat opposite Penny back at the Station House. Clarry had returned home and Exe, thinking that three was, in this instance, most definitely going to be a crowd, had waved away Rory's half-hearted protests and taken his own leave, heading along the platform to the signal box.

Rory looked across at Penny as she sat on the edge of the sofa. Though her green eyes looked tired, she told him she wanted to talk – in truth she was desperate to find out how Rory, though looking a little different, was living here in this remarkable home.

On account, he said, of his having been Removed first, Rory began, telling Penny about everything that had happened since they had last seen other, more than six months ago.

He talked about his Removal; why he thought it had happened; his rescue from the burning car by Clarry; the plastic surgery; how he had found and renovated the station and of the raids on The City he and Exe had planned and completed; why they had done so and, finally, how they had come to be at Gower's clock shop earlier that evening.

Penny had known Rory for three years and throughout that time had become aware that she felt an affinity with, and an attraction to, him, but this man she was listening to now seemed to have been born again. She said: 'I think I am working out this Phoenix thing now...'

Rory looked across at Penny, suddenly realising how much he had missed her, and said, very slightly self-consciously: 'You can blame Clarry for that – it was his idea, but I think I'm kind of stuck with it now.'

Penny smiled at him and said simply: 'I think you should embrace it.'

And then, more quietly: 'Can I stay and help?'

Rory nodded. 'I was rather hoping you'd feel like that,' he admitted. 'After all, it looks like you're stuck out here with us anyway, and you're probably going to need some help in the short term, because the City Police are bound to be looking for you. I'm convinced they didn't bother with me because they were sure I was dead – they're not likely to feel the same way about you.'

Penny agreed; she had had the same thought.

Now it was her turn to tell her story.

'The first thing to say is that I think you're right about it all being to do with Lorna going missing. After you disappeared, I went on looking into it myself.'

'Brave of you,' said Rory. 'Most City people would have just let things be.'

'You didn't.'

'No – and look where it got me!' said Rory.

'Well, I decided to speak to some of her old colleagues at the People Department – I knew Lorna was quite friendly with a couple of them and thought they were probably my only chance of being able to shed any light on what had happened.

'One woman clammed up as soon as I mentioned Lorna – she was just scared stiff and refused point blank to even talk to me. I still don't know if she knew anything or whether she just feared repercussions from being seen talking about Lorna – I guess anyone working in that department is going to understand only too well what it means if a good Citizen simply disappears.

'But the second person I tried was more helpful. At first, he was a bit wary, but he gradually became interested in what I was trying to find out. I eventually managed to persuade him to get me into the department building one night and to help me access Lorna's personnel file to see if there was any indication of where she might have been taken, or why.'

Rory's eyebrows shot up. 'Really? I'm not even going to ask how you persuaded him... he was taking one hell of a risk.'

Penny nodded. 'To be honest, I thought at the time he was just a bit keen on me and would do anything to help, but now I think I was flattering myself. Looking back, it was too good to be true.'

'Hindsight is a wonderful thing. But did it work – did you find anything?'

'I did. He gave me a password for the system which was enough to let me access Lorna's file. I could see the standard biographical details you'd expect, together with information about her career path, earnings and so on. It was stuff I should only really have been able to see if I had worked in the People Department of the People Department, as it were, but there was nothing about her Removal.'

Penny paused for a moment and Rory spoke. 'I'm sensing there is something else though.'

'There is, yes. You see, what I suspect this man didn't realise is that her file still included links to the projects she had been working on and although I didn't have much time, I did find something that looked a bit out of the ordinary.'

'Go on,' urged Rory.

'There was one particular file that caught my eye. It was headed Operation Cuckoo's Nest and had thousands of Citizens' names included on a list.'

Rory frowned. 'Operation Cuckoo's Nest? What's that about? Was there anything significant about the names?'

'Well, at the time I didn't get a chance to get very far into it; my supposed new friend was standing outside in the corridor opening and closing the door every few seconds to let me know that I should hurry up. But the first thing I saw was the name of the lead minister for the project – Byron St John.'

Rory said: 'St John – really? That man again.'

He continued, just as Penny was about to speak: 'Penny, do you have any idea why they should have waited these few months between you going to the department and them Removing you?'

Penny shook her head. 'I don't know what, if anything, finally prompted it, but I was followed by drones most days ever since that night.

'I tried not to let on that I realised but maybe it finally became obvious when I shook off the drones a few times – simply because I was fed-up with being shadowed. Perhaps they thought I was up to something I shouldn't have been.'

'Quite possibly. By the way, you didn't mention the name of the helpful fellow who let you into the department – the one you thought was sweet on you. I take it you remember?' he added, slyly.

Penny pouted. 'Oh, yes, I remember all right, though he had a very ordinary name. It was Richard – Richard Brown.'

Rory stared at her. 'Richard Brown? Well, well. It just gets more and more interesting,' and he proceeded to tell Penny how he too had come across Brown and of his association with Byron St John.

Penny listened, but she was getting twitchy and eventually Rory realised that she was desperate to butt in.

'Sorry, Penny...'

'You didn't let me finish what I was saying... you see, although I didn't get a chance to look at all the names when I was in the People Department, I had gone prepared and I downloaded the file with the list that Lorna had been working on and took it away with me.'

Rory's mouth opened wide. 'What? Why didn't you say something earlier?'

Penny gave him an arch look. 'I would have done – if you'd let me get a word in edgeways! Anyway... not only did I manage to take it away with me, but I have read it thoroughly since – and I smuggled it out with me when I was Removed.'

By now Rory had overcome his pretend indignation and was laughing. 'Quick thinking – and how did you smuggle it out exactly – in your underwear?'

'Actually, that is exactly how I did it, if you must know,' teased

Penny. 'But the question you should have asked me is whose name was on the list.'

Rory fought hard to contain his grin but gave in and asked the question that was expected of him.

'You win: whose name was on it?'

Penny looked him straight in the eyes.

'Yours,' she said.

Rory had called back Clarry and Exe, and asked Roger to join them too, swiftly introducing him to Penny.

He quickly explained to them the basics of what Penny had told him, including the revelation about Richard Brown.

He continued: 'Now, we'd like to tell you a little more about what Penny discovered...'

He inserted into his computer the tiny device Penny had used to download the list from the People Department and they all turned their eyes to the screen. There, first and foremost, was the heading: Operation Cuckoo's Nest.

Beneath it was: Lead Minister: Byron St John.

Penny took over. 'Basically, what we now have is a list of names in A-Z order, by the looks of it all Citizens selected for Removal. I think if we start with the letter A you will see what I mean.'

She selected a page with around 100 surnames, all beginning with the first letter of the alphabet. She clicked on one randomly, a man named Anderson, and up came a page of information.

At the top of this page was Anderson's photograph above his address in The City.

This was followed by three dates.

The first was his date of birth.

The second, which was just over three years after that, was preceded by the word 'Chosen'.

The final date, some four months ago, followed the word 'Removed'.

Clarry, Exe and Roger stared at each other but before any of them could ask a question, Penny continued speaking.

'You will see that there is also a link to another page. But I think we should just quickly jump a few letters before we come to that, if you don't mind?'

At Rory's nod, she continued down the list to K, scrolled to the name Kennet, Rory, and clicked through.

The detailed page came up on the screen.

Rory's picture, address at Templar Court and birthdate was there. The 'Chosen' date was just under four years later. And the Removed date was the exact one that Rory's car, on its way to Workhouse A5, had been blown off the road in an attempt to silence him for good, before he had risen so unexpectedly from its black metallic ashes.

Penny then clicked on the link, which was labelled 'Beneficiary'. It opened a new page headed 'St Peter's, West Harrow.' On that page, Rory's name was included, but it was just one on a long list.

Rory was aware that the other three men were all looking at him, waiting for him to respond. But, for a moment, he said nothing. Although he had, of course, known what was coming, he felt different now that others were present.

His face, usually so expressive, was a mask, unable to raise its customary easy smile. He heard Clarry's deep voice from across the room. 'Rory – what do you think it means? And what on earth's this reference to St Peter's in Harrow all about?'

As Rory remained silent, Exe filled the void, asking the question that Penny herself had already sought an answer to.

'Pen, are you and Lorna Sexton on the list?'

Penny shook her head. 'No, neither of us are on it.'

Roger ran his bony right hand through his right side curtain of hair, a look of supreme irritation on what the others could see of his face.

'Then what is this?' he asked Penny.

'If this is a list of people who have been Removed, why aren't you and Lorna on it? I mean, Lorna's surely been Removed, hasn't she? And you certainly have!'

Roger's indignant response to this affront to what he regarded as the obvious truth was just what Rory needed to snap him out of his silence.

'Penny,' he said. 'Can we have a look at the other names, in case they shed any more light on this?'

'Rory, there are thousands here – we can't check them all now.' This was Clarry, ever mindful of the early start that awaited him just a few hours from now.

'Fair enough – just pick a few names out would you, Penny? Then we can let the old man here go and get his beauty sleep.' He pretended not to notice the grocer's mock scoff from the armchair he was regally occupying.

'Sure,' said Penny, and they looked through another 20 or so names that neither she nor Rory recognised. Information was complete on all but four of them, for whom no Removed date had yet been recorded.

A silence fell over the five.

Penny turned to Rory, asking the same question that Clarry had unsuccessfully sought an answer to earlier. 'Does St Peter's, or West Harrow, mean anything to you?'

He thought for a moment as the others looked at him expectantly. 'Not a thing.'

After a few more seconds, he continued: 'What it seems we have is a long list of people Removed from The City, presumably to some prescribed plan master-minded by Byron St John. But we don't know why so many are suddenly being Removed or why these particular Citizens – me included – were selected. The one other thing we do know from my own case is that this has nothing to do with justice – not even the harsh version of it that is practised in The City these days.'

He stood up, suddenly. 'Look, I think we should make use of this list. Tomorrow, I suggest we head to Harrow, to see if we can pick up any leads there.'

Exe looked over at his old friend. 'Looks like things are about to hot up Clarry,' he said.

Clarry's eyes moved from Rory's face, which had a determined look on it, back to Exe.

'About bloody time,' he said.

Chapter 13

THE CHURCH

Rory, Exe and Penny stood on the pavement beside a 6ft high hedge that separated the tidy grounds of St Peter's Church in West Harrow from one of the suburban streets that it sat in the middle of.

On both sides of the relatively small church building stood a row of semi-detached houses synonymous with the Metroland era, when developers had built streets of family homes to keep pace with the expanding railways leading in and out of the capital, creating a set of thriving suburbs that, for decades, had become both economic success stories and safe spaces to bring up children.

Now The City was the be-all and end-all, these old suburbs were merely a geographical halfway point between that centre of affluence and the poorer, more simple life of the Outside.

Those who lived here were no better off than the rest of the Outsiders – they were just physically closer to what they could not have.

Though that meant shorter commutes for those who worked there, it also made the divide seem worse.

From the high ground of the hill in whose shadow St Peter's

stood it was possible to see the golden City laid out in front of you – close enough to almost smell the riches that were denied you.

Standing on the pavement, Rory looked both left and right along the street that was so typical of its type.

The red-brick houses, built a century ago, had been marketed at the time as suburban villas, with their own front and back gardens; the perfect places to buy.

They had looked alike, bringing a smart, semi-formal uniformity to the business of home-making and child-rearing in more innocent times.

Those front lawns had been proudly looked after (God forbid you didn't mow yours every Sunday) to make sure the owners at the very least kept up with the Joneses next door.

Now those tidy little patches of green had, in the main, been obliterated by waves of concrete.

These had been laid down in the mistaken belief that the motor car was the future for ever and that lush front gardens were less important than the urgent need to park your own car in front of your own front door – even though that same chunk of petrol-propelled, coloured metal was slowly and insidiously polluting the lungs of the little children being so carefully nurtured indoors.

As he stood there, something was nagging away on the edges of Rory's brain. It was annoying him greatly because he couldn't quite get hold of what it was. It was as though he could see himself as a child, pushing away at a door, trying to open it, but that door was getting stuck before it would open more than a crack.

He frowned.

'Everything all right Rory?' It was Exe who spoke.

Rory was snapped out of his contemplation. 'Yes, fine thanks; sorry. I was just thinking there was something familiar about this place; yet I don't understand how it could be so. It's slightly unsettling, that's all. Let's go and have a look round, shall we?'

He headed decisively in the direction of one of the low wooden gates that led into the grounds of the church, stooping very slightly to push it open.

Between the hedge and the church was a patch of grass on which a group of half a dozen children had set up some cricket stumps and were playing vigorously and noisily. They were using a tennis ball; though the evidence of a broken pane of glass in the windows of the low, more modern extension to the church they played alongside indicated that perhaps they had not always done so.

Rory's frown had been changed to a smile by that thought as the three of them walked past the young bowlers and batters and on towards the church.

Despite the stylish grandeur of the building itself, the door that served as the main entrance on a day-to-day basis was small and unobtrusive, hidden away semi-apologetically to one side of the church.

Rory led the way inside, and the three of them were immediately struck by the sense of tranquillity that everyone finds entering a house of God, whether they are a believer or not. Rory didn't know what it was that did it; perhaps it was the sheer age of the place and the knowledge of all the changes it had stood through; but a sense of calm overtook him as he looked up and down the nave.

Very quietly at first, there came the sound of an organ playing. Rory had the feeling someone had been waiting until the door was opened before beginning to play. Religion wasn't practised in The City, and he had no idea what the piece was, but it felt right for the space; it had what he considered to be a spiritual feel. It gradually filled the church.

The trio stood, listening and looking around them, as the music surrounded them before building to a crescendo and then fading away.

A man stepped out from an alcove to the left of the nave, opening both arms in greeting.

He was a small, white man, slim and dapper. He wore no cassock but was dressed plainly in a dark grey suit which fitted his svelte shape as though he been born wearing it. His hair was grey and thinning though neatly cut and his eyes, they saw as he approached, were a pale blue, almost translucent. It was difficult to be sure of his age. The lines on his face suggested at least 60 but the wiriness of his body belied that possibility.

'Welcome to our church,' he said, in an unassuming quiet voice that nonetheless held their attention immediately.

'I am the Reverend William Faraday. I don't believe I have had the pleasure of seeing any of you here before?'

Rory coughed, slightly nervously. His lack of religious knowledge left him unsure even of the correct term of address to this churchman.

He decided to stay safely secular. 'Sir,' he began, 'I hope you don't mind us coming to see you, but we were wondering if you might be able to help us with some research we are carrying out.'

The Reverend Faraday considered both the request and the man in front of him for a moment.

'Are you from The City?' he asked.

Rory thought quickly – this was not a question he had envisaged. He decided honesty would be the best policy.

'I used to be. I'm not anymore,' he said.

The little vicar raised a perfectly tailored eyebrow quizzically. 'Removed?' he asked.

Rory inclined his head and pressed his thin lips together. 'I'm afraid so,' he answered.

'Well, you don't look like a desperado.' The Reverend Faraday smiled. 'But I'm going to take you at your word. Forgive my slight reticence, you must remember that The City is no friend to organised religion so I naturally must be a little cautious when someone visits who appears to be cut of that particular cloth.'

'We do understand,' said Rory, before going on to introduce both himself and Exe and Penny. 'Penny,' he explained, 'has also recently been Removed.'

The Reverend Faraday looked intrigued, but said he was pleased to meet them all. 'Come with me,' he added. 'Then we can discuss this research you would like some help with.'

He led the way down the nave, past the pulpit and towards a door in the corner. The trio followed him, led by Rory, and they found themselves in a spacious room.

'Take a seat in here,' he said to them. 'Would you all like some coffee?'

As he had instinctively done with so many of his new friends, Rory had taken an instant liking to this efficient, welcoming man who had an aura of high intelligence to go alongside his evident humanity. 'Thank you, sir, that would be very welcome, and kind of you,' he said.

The Reverend William Faraday smiled in a way that seemed to add extra colour to his incredibly pale eyes.

'Shall we dispense with the formality?' he suggested. 'William is my name – I'll be very happy if you'll just call me that.'

He left the room in his quiet fashion to make the drinks.

The four of them now sat around the table, each with a mug of coffee in front of them, as Rory told William the story of how he and Penny had both come to be Removed from The City and what they had since discovered that had led them to the church.

At first, he felt a little uncomfortable as he outlined the rather less than lawful methods the three of them had used at various points of their operations.

The Reverend Faraday sensed his discomfort.

He said: 'Rory, please do not feel the need to apologise for what you have done.

'I answer to a higher authority than The City government and my view of what is just and what is not may well be a little different to theirs.'

They all laughed and, from that moment, all four of them relaxed and Rory felt he had more than just the one extra man sitting next to him on his side.

William said: 'I think, if we are trying to find out how your name came to be linked with this parish Rory, that what we need to do is to look at our parish records, which include all the births, deaths and marriages that were registered here.

'When these records were first made, they would have been kept at a register office elsewhere but paper records from the past were sent to the parishes some time ago rather than being destroyed when everything went digital. Let's see what we have. In what year were you born, Rory?'

Rory told him and the vicar crossed the floor to a long row of shelves on which stood an unexpectedly clean set of books, ledgers and folders of various sizes.

He went straight to one area, his fingers tracing along a series of folders until he alighted on one.

'I thought as much; this is what we have for you,' he said, pulling the folder from the shelf and handing it to Rory.

Rory opened the manila folder that had the year of his birth printed in large numerals on the outside flap and pulled out the papers within. He was surprised that there was so little dust – he could hardly believe that there was much call from people to be looking through them. But the whole of the inside of William Faraday's church was spotless; it seemed whoever cleaned did a thorough job of everything.

He saw that all the documents were in date order – another testament to the reverend's fastidiousness – and quickly found the date of his birthday stamped on the front of an A4-sized buff envelope.

He glanced across at Exe and Penny who were both sat opposite him across the table.

His fingers were very slightly unsteady as they touched the top of the envelope. The flap was folded over but the gum had long since failed and it was no longer stuck down. Rory opened it, extracting a sheet of thick, cream-coloured paper.

The others did their best to contain their impatience as Rory read down. That he had found something of interest was evident by the slight widening of his intelligent eyes, but they knew better than to rush him.

Rory put down the paper on the table in front of him. He looked up at his two friends again. He swivelled the paper round so that it could be read from the other side of the desk and pushed it towards Exe and Penny.

'So, what do you make of that then?' he asked.

They both read the entry at the same time.

January 31. Born in the Parish of St Peter, West Harrow: Rory John (Boy) to Kenneth (Railwayman) and Annette Kennet (Housewife) of 136 Drury Road.

At the foot of the page was the signature of one Trevor Winter, the incumbent vicar of the parish at the time, and a predecessor of the Reverend William Faraday, whose confirmed acknowledgement of the birth appeared to make it official in the eyes of the church.

It was Exe, who had the knack of broaching the questions no-one else felt able to ask, who came straight to the point.

'What do you think this means then Rev?' he said, irreverently.

William Faraday smiled. He found the informality of Rory's tall companion somewhat refreshing.

He looked around the table at the three of them.

'You are all intelligent people. I think you will have already realised what it means. This record shows that Rory here was born to a couple who lived just a few streets away from this place.

'What this document proves beyond any doubt, Rory, is what you probably already suspect … that not only are you an Outsider now, but that you always were one.'

Chapter 14

THE SUBURBAN DREAM

Leaving the Reverend William Faraday behind in his church, having swapped information about how they could keep in touch with each other, Rory, Exe and Penny walked along the suburban streets of West Harrow.

Drury Road, where Kenneth and Annette Kennet had been living when Rory was born, proved to be a lengthy residential street not far from St Peter's.

Many of the houses were terraced but were big enough to have three or four bedrooms each and they still retained their stoic grace.

The trio stood outside the wooden gate that led to number 136. The gate itself badly needed a new coat of the green paint that had last been applied many years back. The areas where paint had flaked off showed that it had previously been painted black.

Beyond the gate was a short path of black and white tiles that was in need of a clean and a good sweep. A combination of fallen leaves, dirt and wind-blown rubbish had created a slowly decaying layer of mush.

Rory stood with his right hand on the gate and looked up at

the first-floor windows of the house in front of him. The glass was intact and yellowing net curtains hung at them all, keeping the secrets of this once proud Edwardian villa from prying eyes. The ground floor, likewise, was hidden behind a nylon mask.

As he stood in front of the house, Rory experienced a moment of light-headedness and swayed for a second, putting out his left hand to clutch the top of the gate, ensuring he maintained his equilibrium.

'All right Rory?' Exe asked. The man had a remarkable ability to spot Rory's little moments.

Rory smiled, some colour returning to the cheeks that had become pallid just seconds earlier.

'All good,' he murmured.

'You know this place too, don't you?' It was the inexorable Exe again.

Rory drew in a deep breath, before breathing out through his nose. 'I think so, Exe, but I still don't remember it. I have no clue when I was here or what happened here. But, yes, I have been here before. That's all I do know.'

Gritting his teeth, he pushed open the gate, using some force as it was stuck in position by the garden debris.

Led by Rory, the three of them walked up the little path to the front door, which was surrounded by a wooden porch. A doorbell was positioned just below head height to the right of the front door and, with a determined push of his right index finger, Rory pressed it.

Silence met his efforts, so instead he used the mottled, silver-coloured door knocker in the hope of rousing anyone who might be inside. Again, there was no response.

This time it was Penny who spoke. 'Looking at the condition of the place, I'd say there's unlikely to be anyone living here at the moment, Rory.'

He knew she was right. 'Yes. Let's move on to the neighbours.'

The house next door was similar in stature, but there the similarities ended. It was not only clearly occupied but also very well upkept. Although areas of the brickwork and pointing showed some need of attention, it was obvious to all that much tender loving care went in to keeping the wood and paintwork looking smart, that the windows were cleaned regularly and the path was swept.

Not only that, but the owners had never succumbed to the peer pressure that would have necessitated digging up their front garden to provide a driveway. Instead, a square patch of green fronted the house, surrounded by neat borders in which pretty flowers provided a colourful reminder that houseproud folk still existed in these forgotten suburbs.

This looked promising. The house was well cared for and had an established garden. Perhaps, thought Rory, there might be people here who had been around 25-30 years ago who would remember the Kennet family and, maybe, even know where they might be found now, or what had happened to them.

Again, he stepped up to the front door and rang the doorbell. This time, he heard it chime within the villa and seconds later he heard a door being opened and the sound of shuffling feet coming along the hallway.

The voice of an elderly man came from the other side of the

front door. 'Hello? Who's there?'

Rory took a moment before replying.

'Hello, I'm very sorry to bother you – my name is Rory and I'm trying to find out some information about a family who used to live next door to you, at number 136. I wonder if you'd be kind enough to help me – I have two friends with me as well,' he added, not wanting the old man to be surprised if he were to open the door.

There seemed, however, no immediate prospect of that.

'Who is it you're asking about?' came the voice from the other side of the door. 'There hasn't been anyone living next door for a very long time now.'

Rory realised he was going to have to work if he was to persuade the man to open the door to him.

He said: 'The family's name was Kennet and I'm really keen to trace them if I possibly can. I know they lived here between 25 and 30 years ago...'

The voice from within cut him off in mid-flow. 'I'm very sorry, young man, but I don't know anything about them. I can't help you. I can't help you...' and with that Rory heard the old man turn round a lot more quickly than he had approached and firmly close the door to the living room or whichever part of the house he had earlier emerged from.

There was a very definite finality to the move. But Rory was determined to try again – because there was a note of panic in the householder's voice that made him certain that the old boy had been scared when he heard the Kennet family name – and that he had lied about knowing them.

His companions felt it too. As Rory turned round, with a slightly rueful look on his face, Penny stepped in. 'He was lying,' she said simply. Exe nodded his agreement.

'Yes,' confirmed Rory. 'He panicked when he heard the name. Why should he do that? We're going to have to try again but I don't think now is the moment. Let's give him an hour or two and then come back to see if he has got over whatever bothered him so much.'

Which was exactly what they did, and by being patient they had a stroke of luck. As the three of them approached the house 90 minutes later, they saw that the front door was open and, as they reached the gate, a tidy-looking old lady with short grey hair came through the doorway with a small plant in each hand.

She looked up at the sound of the gate being unlatched. Rory prepared to plead with her not to turn tail and run back into the house, but he need not have worried.

The lady of the house smiled at them and immediately addressed Rory, who was at the front of the queue.

'Hello! Are you the people who my husband sent away a little while ago?' Her tone was unexpectedly friendly after the rather scuttling nature of the welcome they had received from the elderly man earlier.

Rory turned on his full beam smile. It was known to work well with older ladies. 'That was us,' he confirmed. 'I'm afraid we rather caught your husband unawares. He seemed a little perturbed; I am sorry if we startled him. I promise you we mean you no harm.'

The lady laughed and shook her handsome grey head. 'Anything out of his routines perturbs my husband these days, he's got a bit too used to only having me for company and he doesn't get out and about much anymore. His eyesight is failing him a bit – it's hit his confidence,' she added, feeling perhaps she was being a little disloyal.

Sensing that full-beam Rory was about to overdo it, Penny spoke up. 'That's quite all right, we really do understand – you can't often get strangers pitching up at your front door. But would it be at all possible to ask you a few questions – about the people who used to live next door?'

The lady put down her plant pots on the edge of the well-tended lawn and beckoned them into the garden.

'Of course it is. Please follow me,' she said and led the way into the house.

Having introduced herself as Celia Millan, she called out to her husband (John) and offered tea and biscuits all round as they settled themselves in the well-proportioned and comfortably furnished living room.

John soon joined them. His apologies for his earlier attitude were waved away by Rory, Penny and Exe, who reiterated that they understood. John continued: 'We don't really get many callers you see, and Celia had just popped out to get those plants you saw her with. I'm afraid I get a little nervous when I'm here on my own these days.'

It was Celia herself who opened the conversation proper though.

'So, what is it you'd like to ask?' she said.

Rory waded in. 'We are trying to find out some more about the Kennet family, who we believe lived next door to you at number 136 – the empty house as it is now. We think they would have lived there, maybe 25 to 30 years ago. Do you remember them at all?'

And then he quickly added: 'I suppose I ought to confirm first that you were actually living here yourselves then?'

Celia laughed again. 'Oh yes, we were here all right.'

She looked across at John who was appearing a little uneasy again. 'It's OK, darling,' she said, replying to his unasked question. 'After all this time, I think we are safe to talk about it.' The old man nodded, appearing soothed by his wife's answer, and the certainty in her voice.

'Go on then, you tell them,' he said, softly.

Celia looked up at her guests, each of them sitting on the edges of their respective seats with a bone china cup of tea perched on their knee, the arm of the chair or a side table.

'Yes, we were here,' repeated Celia.

Then she looked at Rory and said: 'And I rather think you were too, weren't you?'

Rory stared back across the room.

'What makes you think that?' he asked.

Celia stood up and went across to an antique bureau that stood in one corner of the room. She opened the pull-down front and took out a photo album whose leather cover had seen better days but had been handled down the decades with much affection.

Without speaking, she walked back across the room to Rory and opened the album. Her strong, thin fingers leafed through half a dozen pages until she came to the photographs she was seeking.

She turned the album round so that it was the right way up for Rory to see and, as both Penny and Exe set their cups of tea down and moved swiftly to Rory's side, Celia pointed to the photograph on the top outside edge of the left-hand page of the album.

The colour print showed a man in early middle age standing proudly in a long, thin ribbon of back garden, with vegetable plots and a greenhouse behind him. One step in front of him, with his little hands resting against his hips in a proud pose, was a young boy with a huge smile on his face.

Despite his tender age, it was very obviously a young Rory.

As Penny laid her hand upon his shoulder, Rory felt tears welling up in his eyes and he closed them, trying to rid himself of the unwanted show of emotion. He tried looking away, but his eyes were drawn back to the photo album that Celia still held in front of him.

Beneath the first picture she had indicated was another and on the page opposite two more. The young Rory appeared in them all. In one he was alone – except for a garden gnome ornament for company. In another, he appeared with the middle-aged man again and in the last with the man and three others – a woman with blonde, shoulder-length hair, and a well-dressed couple who were clearly Celia and John.

Unable to help himself, Rory wiped tears from his face with the back of his left hand. He tried to speak, but struggled to get the words out and gave up the struggle, shaking his head and continuing to blink away the tears that kept coming as he stared, with intent, at the dark red carpet on the Millans' floor.

This time, it was John's quiet voice that he heard.

'I'm sorry that you've been upset, Rory. But you can see that it is you in the photographs. Even I can see it. I knew who you were as soon as I looked through the spyhole in the front door when you came by earlier.'

Penny answered for Rory. 'We thought we knew that next door might have been Rory's home at one point, and that is what brought us here. But what we don't know is what happened to the family – do you know anything at all about that?'

Celia had gone to sit down, leaving the photo album on Rory's lap as he composed himself again. She looked at Penny shrewdly before speaking.

'We know a little,' she admitted. 'That little we know is the reason John was so worried about talking to you – even after all this time. You see, we had it made clear to us that we were not to speak of what happened to anyone – ever. But in nearly 30 years, no-one has ever come knocking; no-one has ever come asking – until you, today.'

By now, Rory had got a grip on his emotions and, with Penny and Exe still standing either side of his chair, he felt able to re-enter the conversation which, after all, concerned him more than most.

'Please tell us what you know. Anything at all. I'm sure there is no reason to be afraid, not after all this time.'

John again looked at Celia, seeking reassurance. His wife nodded and her kind eyes gave the old man the confidence to speak as Rory, Penny and Exe waited expectantly.

'Well, as you know, Ken and Annie were our neighbours. We had already been here about ten years when they moved in next door and, although they were a bit younger than us, we quickly became good friends. Both Ken and I used to love tending our gardens and we would speak over the fence a lot, and Celia and Annie often went out shopping together into the town. When Annie became pregnant with you, Rory, we were delighted for them. We hadn't been able to have any children of our own, sadly, so after you were born we used to enjoy seeing you out and about in the garden and the street, and we even babysat you from time to time whenever Ken and Annie wanted a night out.

'For a couple of years, everything was perfect. Your mum and dad were so happy together, and with you, and they were the nicest neighbours we could ever have hoped for. Life here was just fine. The City wasn't the big deal then that it is now, and there was still enough work and money around here to keep us all living to a nice standard without worrying too much about the future.'

John stopped talking and gulped in some air.

'And then, of course, everything changed.'

Celia got up from her chair and walked across the room again, this time past Rory and the others until she was at her husband's side. But John looked up at her, tears in his eyes now, and shook his head slightly.

Celia took over.

'You had just started at the local nursery school that was run by the church, Rory. Ken and Annie came and shared with us all the little updates about you in those first few months, because they were so proud of everything that you were doing. Unfortunately, things then became more difficult.'

Rory felt an emptiness in his chest.

He said: 'Please tell me what happened, Celia.'

She nodded her head, though Rory could tell that she too was finding this painful. Eventually, she steeled herself and the explanation, when it came, was almost blurted out.

'It all started to change after your father, Ken, lost his job. As The City began to grow in influence, a lot of the local, traditional jobs out here were lost. Ken struggled to find anything else and as the money dried up, we knew that Ken and Annie were struggling. We offered to help them out but, of course, they were too proud to accept any help from us.

'Then, one day a few months later, officials from The City came to the house. And they took you away, Rory.

'Your parents were given no choice, they were forced to give you up and move away to a different area to start a new life. We never found out where they went.

'We only know what we do because your mother was brave enough to slip out and tell me what was happening whilst The City officials waited outside to move them. But one of them must have suspected something because they came in to see us afterwards and warned us never to say anything about the family next door to anyone, no matter what.

'They told us that your parents were being moved for their own safety because of some unspecified threat to them, and we just pretended that we believed them – I didn't want to risk dropping poor Annie in it.

'That was the last we ever heard of them. And, until today, it was the last we ever heard or saw of you too.'

Rory sat back in his armchair, feeling as though he been battered about the head with his own emotions. The truth about where he had come from and what had happened to him was only just beginning to sink in and he felt as though he needed much more time to really begin to understand any of it.

It was left to Penny to ask: 'Celia, do you know why Rory was taken away?'

The proud old lady shook her head. 'We were never told, and we never found out. Within months it became clear that The City was becoming ever more powerful, and that life out here was going to change. It didn't do to go asking questions of anyone to do with it. Its power and influence just grew and grew and life for the rest of us stood still for a while and then started to go backwards. I guess that was inevitable.

'People around here quickly worked out that the only sure way of getting paid enough to live on was to commute in to work in menial jobs there. So that became the way life was. Here we are, more than 25 years later, at our age just living out our time as well as we can using up the savings we had managed to put aside all those years ago when we both worked. But despite it all, we're happy. We still have each other.'

She gazed down at her husband, who sat in his chair, nodding his head.

'Yes,' he echoed. 'We still have each other.'

Chapter 15

WINTER'S TALE

The Reverend William Faraday sat in his car contemplating the visit he was about to make. He looked across the sparse, untidy communal swathe of grass that separated the side of the road from the drab, characterless terrace of houses and sighed.

He had already been there for five minutes and he remained in the vehicle for another couple before, finally, making up his mind. He got out, locked the car, looked around and started to walk at a slow pace across the 'green', which was really yellow-brown and looked more like a piece of diseased wasteland than the verdant play area it had originally been intended to be.

The 1960s-built row of concrete houses was even less attractive. Built at the time that council house building was seen as the way forward, it was dull, unattractive and depressing.

The sort of place you go to disappear.

Or to die, disillusioned, forgotten and unloved.

William approached the front door of the third house from the left in the terrace.

A kitchen window next to the door was slightly open and an age-stained net curtain billowed momentarily from it as a gust of wind got up before its folds settled back again.

William knocked gently on the glass pane of the door. He heard light footsteps from the kitchen to the left and a latch was turned on the inside of the door. From the gap between the edge of the door and the frame, the small, thin face of a woman in her 70s peered out.

'Oh vicar, it's you,' said the woman as she saw the dapper man in his well-fitting grey suit standing on the doorstep.

'Hello, Mrs Stanley, and how are you?' asked William, in his visiting-the-parishioners voice.

'Same as usual, thanks vicar,' said the housekeeper, opening the door to admit the clergyman.

'And how is he?'

Mrs Stanley took a second or two before answering.

'I think 'fading' is the word I'd use vicar,' she said resignedly.

William nodded. 'Has the doctor been recently?'

Mrs Stanley replied: 'I don't think there's anything a doctor could do for him vicar. There's nothing new wrong with his body. I think he's just had enough. It's sad to see it in a man who was once so strong and so full of life. In a way I'm glad his old parishioners can't see him now – he was that popular back in the day, it would break their hearts I think. Instead, it's him that's broken – a broken man. He has been for near 30 years,' and Mrs Stanley shook her little bird-like, grey head in sorrow.

Acknowledging her with a light hand on her right shoulder, William moved through into the house.

As a result of the ministrations of the faithful Mrs Stanley, it remained clean, though the sparseness and age of its furnishings lent it a melancholy air.

In the magnolia-painted sitting room, William found his predecessor, the Reverend Trevor Winter, seated in a worn armchair of an indeterminate colour, a pair of cream antimacassars covering up the grubbiness of the arms.

Two long, thin, bony hands gripped the pieces of cloth as though the old man was clinging on for dear life. William could see the veins standing out in the almost translucent backs of his hands.

'Ah William,' came a voice from deep within the chair, and a shock of thick white hair could be seen as he sat forward, his hands still gripping the covered arms, 'how nice to see you again. It has been a little while, has it not?'

'A couple of months, no more than that,' replied William, seating himself on a plain pine chair that he moved from next to the wall so that he was sat opposite the man he had come to see.

'Would you like some tea, vicars?' asked Mrs Stanley, checking in on them.

'Tea?' said the Reverend Winter. 'Oh yes, yes please, Mrs Stanley. Make a pot if you would, then we can share it between us.'

The housekeeper nodded her head, closed the door of the sitting room, and went off to the kitchen to put the kettle on.

While they waited for her to return, the two most recent custodians of St Peter's Church looked at each other. An atmosphere of mutual respect and friendship was evident between them.

'I sense there may be a reason you have come to see me today, William,' said the older man quietly.

A little smile played on the Reverend William Faraday's lips. 'You always could see through anybody, Trevor.'

The old man's face lit up for a moment. 'Yes, yes. Well, people were my business for a long time, William. As they are yours now. But that was all a long time ago, wasn't it? We both know that, and we both know why,' and with that, the little flicker of life that had inflected his voice waned.

William said thoughtfully: 'That's why I've come to see you.'

'Yes,' said the old vicar. 'I hoped it might be.'

The Reverend Winter's hands relaxed, releasing a handful of cloth from each.

He waited while Mrs Stanley brought in and set out the tea, took a sip from his little off-white cup with yellow daisies painted on it, allowed the housekeeper time to leave the room again and then turned his eyes to William's.

It was the latter who spoke first. 'I think it's time to tell the truth. There are some people I wish to speak to, and when I tell you who one of them is, I believe you will understand why.'

Winter sighed. 'If only you knew what a relief this will be for me, William, you wouldn't even need to ask. After all these years of hiding away from what I did, I long to be released from my shame and from my guilt.'

The younger man shook his head. 'You know I think you are being too hard on yourself. It wasn't your fault, Trevor.'

The white-haired man opposite him raised a resigned smile.

'We've been through this, William. Time and again. It was my fault. I believed them when they said all they wanted to do was offer the orphans a better life. I believed them – and I gave my blessing to the idea.'

'You were guilty of nothing but trying to do your best for

disadvantaged children,' replied William. 'You weren't to know what was to follow.'

The Reverend Winter continued as though he hadn't heard his friend's interruption. 'And then they took all those other children as well – tearing them from their families; breaking those parents' hearts into little pieces and scattering their love to the four winds. I allowed that to happen, William – me.'

William Faraday put down his teacup.

He insisted: 'You weren't to blame, Trevor. The Church supported the idea too, don't forget – they believed that what The City was doing was for the best. You were only going along with what you were told.'

The Reverend Winter looked over the rim of his own cup at the friend who had supported him ever since he had taken over from him at St Peter's nearly three decades earlier.

'Yes, but I helped identify the families they took the children from. I thought they were going to get help. I found out afterwards that they paid us for them, William. They actually paid the Church a sum of money which was then handed out to parishes based on how many children from each had been taken. Can you conceive of such wickedness?'

The old man shook his head, the sorrow evident in his faded eyes. Slowly, he gathered his thoughts again.

'Tell me about these people William. I'd like to know who has finally persuaded you that the time is right to tell the truth.'

William explained about the visit he had received from Rory; about how he had been Removed from The City – and about the list that Penny had stolen from the People Department.

He concluded: 'I still don't plan to tell anyone about your part in it, Trevor, but I would like your permission to tell them at least some of what happened and why. They need to understand that in order to tackle this properly, and to know what they might be up against when they do.'

The Reverend Winter took another sip of tea and settled back in his armchair, his head resting on its greasy, threadbare back.

'Oh, you have my permission to do that, William, you really do. I have something else that may help you too. Something you should give to these young people. I don't trust The City, you see, as I am sure you will understand.'

William nodded his head. 'I understand only too well. But what is it you have that you think could help?'

The old man pointed a long and crooked finger in the direction of a battered sideboard across the room.

'Open the second drawer of that, will you, William?'

William did as bid. Inside the drawer was a single A4 sized brown envelope.

He drew it out and handed it over to his elderly predecessor, who lifted the flap and took from it a paperclipped sheaf of paper than ran to several dozen pages.

With unsteady hands the Reverend Winter slowly leafed through the pages until he found the one he was looking for. He looked down and pointed towards the foot of the page, making sure William could see what he was indicating.

'If it wasn't for the fact that one shouldn't gamble, I'd have a little wager with you, William, that this differs slightly from the list that your new friends have.'

For a moment, even the cool, calm and collected William was nonplussed as he looked down at Reverend Winter's list and his pale blue eyes widened before contracting again.

He said: 'Is this definitely correct?'

Trevor inclined his head. 'Oh yes, William. Believe me, there is no doubt.' A thin, tired smile played on his grey lips. 'There – you have my last contribution. Please take the papers with you when you go. I have done as much as I am able to now.'

William stood, not insulted by the de facto dismissal from his weary, old friend, and called to Mrs Stanley that he was about to leave.

As the incumbent Vicar of St Peter's was ushered out a minute later by the faithful housekeeper, the Reverend Trevor Winter looked over once more to the sideboard across the room from where he was sitting, and his eyes settled on a bottle of pills that sat on top if it.

He sighed, his mind made up.

Chapter 16

THE SHORTAGE

Having considered how much to reveal about what he knew, the Reverend William Faraday arrived at the Station House where he had arranged to meet Rory, Penny and Exe.

To begin with, the vicar remained silent, listening gravely to the story that Rory told and he was about to speak when an alarm indicated that someone was approaching the station.

Exe moved across to the screen which showed live CCTV images of various areas around the property. 'It's only Clarry,' he said.

The four of them waited for the timely Mr Lionheart to join them, and Rory introduced him to William and explained to him everything they had discovered, first at St Peter's and then at the house of Celia and John, his parents' friends and neighbours.

Clarry was outraged and got to his feet to vent his feelings about the way Rory had been taken from his family.

William calmed him down and then said: 'So now we know what happened to Rory, but I have discovered a lot more about what lay behind it that I can tell you.'

The grocer sat down and waved a thick hand in the clergy-man's direction. 'Then don't let me stop you, vicar,' he said.

The Reverend William Faraday was used to being the centre of attention in his own church, and he was used to larger (though not always much larger) congregations, but he couldn't recall the last time he had had an audience that was hanging on his every word as much as these four were.

And he began with a lie.

'I have been speaking to a number of my fellow clergy; in particular a few who have been around for quite a long time and whose knowledge I thought might be relevant to the subject we are interested in. I thought they might, possibly, be able to shed some light on what happened all those years ago. They were, after all, very involved with their communities.

'It wasn't easy to get them to talk as they only know what they do because some individuals had told them things in confidence – almost on a confessional basis you might say – and such confidences are difficult for men and women of the cloth to break, no matter how distressing the subject matter.'

He looked up. As he had anticipated, four pairs of eyes were trained on him relentlessly.

At this stage, the vicar reverted to the whole truth.

'Between 25 and 30 years ago, when The City was just establishing its dominance over the rest of the country, the focus on the individual, hard work and constant entertainment led to a rapid falling-off in the birth rate.

'The then Finance Director realised that if something wasn't done quickly to correct the situation, The City would find itself in a position in just a single generation's time when there would not be enough working age taxpayers to comfortably pay for all of the services The City would need.

'This would mean that all The Board's plans – and to be fair to them, unlike governments in the old days, they do have long-term plans – would become unaffordable.

'They called this crisis The Shortage and came up with a scheme to increase the birth rate which, as you may know, became the official breeding programme in which some Citizens are paid by the state to have children.

'Once these children are born, the birth mother usually passes them on to be brought up in specially trained foster families, so they are raised in an approved fashion – unless she has been so trained herself of course and wishes to keep them.

'At the age of 12 the children go to live in residential schools where they continue their education and gain a full understanding of the way life in The City works. The idea is that they are all ready to become useful, money-making Citizens by the time they leave school.

'But The Board also realised that the breeding programme would take time to set up so they would need to have more working age contributors sooner than it would take for the programme to start bearing fruit.

'So, as what you found out today corroborates, they decided to bring into The City young children from the Outside. It is now clear that Rory was one of those. They planned to raise them as if they were natural-born Citizens, never revealing to them the truth.'

Penny asked: 'How did they choose the children, William?'

'They began by taking in orphans from the Outside, the idea

being that it would solve The City's problems whilst also doing some good for both the children themselves and the orphanages on the Outside, all of which were at the time struggling to cope with the numbers of children they had to look after.'

'But Rory wasn't an orphan,' pointed out Exe.

'No,' replied William. 'He wasn't. I did say that The City began by taking in orphans. But there were not enough to make the required difference. So, the decision was made to expand what you might call the recruitment programme.'

'And what was the criteria used, William, do you know?' asked Rory, quietly.

'I am told that The City's representatives approached families who were struggling either financially or emotionally to bring up their children. They sought to persuade the parents that the children would have a better life in The City than the families would be able to provide them.

'That may possibly have been true but, as you can probably imagine, the number of families this idea appealed to, even if they were in financial hardship, was incredibly small.

'And this is where things began to take a more sinister turn. Realising that the policy was not going to succeed through persuasion alone, The City decided to enforce it instead.

'So, all the families it had identified had their children taken from them to ensure The City met its quotas. The families were compensated financially and made to move away and start a new life with more money in their pockets. They were told never to return to their original homes and not to contact anyone there.

'The policy was also kept largely quiet inside The City. I don't know how many people knew about it, but I suspect only those who were involved were told, and probably even many of those didn't know the full story – my understanding is all the foster parents, for example, still believed they were taking in orphans.'

William stopped talking, indicating that he had concluded his revelations for now.

He was met by silence.

It was Exe who broke it.

'Good God,' he said, expressing in one short, pithy phrase what the others were all feeling, before adding: 'Sorry, Rev.'

Rory, who had been listening carefully, said: 'Well, that certainly explains a lot.'

He then asked a question that had been worrying him.

'William, the parish link on the list that Penny stole that led us to St Peter's was headed 'Beneficiary'. Do you know what was meant by that?'

The vicar shook his head. 'That I cannot tell you, Rory.'

'Cannot? Or will not?'

'Are they not the same thing?'

There was a moment's silence. Rory looked as though he was wrestling with a retort, but stopped himself and instead said calmly: 'Forgive me, William, but there is something else I must ask you.'

The vicar said: 'Go ahead.'

Rory said: 'What you have given us is a very comprehensive account of what happened – one that you say you have gathered in just a few hours. I won't ask how you really know about all this, because you obviously have your reasons for not telling us. And I might be wrong, but I get the feeling you have a lot of knowledge about things that go on inside The City. I've not yet come across another Outsider who seems to know so much about things they probably shouldn't know anything about. Am I right?'

The Reverend William Faraday smiled slightly. 'Suspicious of me, Rory? Me, a man of God and all?'

Rory shook his head firmly. 'Not suspicious, William. Curious, perhaps. Intrigued, definitely.'

The vicar, whose timing had been well honed at the pulpit, took a moment.

He looked around at everyone else in the room and then admitted: 'Yes, you are right. The truth is, I do know rather a lot more about The City and the way that it works than you might expect me to, because, like you and Penny, I used to live there.'

There was a stunned silence before Exe said: 'Don't tell us you were Removed too, Rev?'

The vicar smiled. 'Not exactly, no. I chose to Remove myself, if you must know.

'As you can probably imagine from my age, I was already living there when politics started to change and The City as we now know it was born. If truth be told, I never felt entirely comfortable with it.

'Over time, I became more and more disillusioned, particularly at the way any sort of spiritual life was being eradicated.

'I realised that there is only room for one religion in The City – and that is money. I wanted something different. So I decided to leave.

'I built myself a new life on the Outside, rather as Rory has begun to do. And I found I rather liked it.'

The four stared at the vicar. It was Rory who responded first. He said: 'You're a dark one, William. I must say that I'm glad you're on our side in all of this.'

There was a murmur of assent from the others.

Then Rory continued: 'I think we can now safely assume that the names on Penny's list are the children originally taken to The City from the Outside.

'And though what William has told us confirms why the children, including me, were taken in the first place, the one thing it doesn't explain is why, now, The City has suddenly decided to Remove us.'

William coughed, mildly. 'So far I can only think of one realistic explanation for it – that this is some form of deliberate social cleansing, though what has prompted it now, after all these years, I do not know.'

He took some sheets of paper from an envelope that was lying in front of him on the coffee table. 'I do have one other piece of information that I think you ought to know.'

There was an expectant hush as he leafed through the papers that the Reverend Winter had entrusted him with earlier.

He said: 'I hope you will understand that I am not able to say exactly where I got this from, but this is the original list of children who were taken from this sector of the Outside to The City all those years ago.

'Rory's name is on it. But if you care to check it against the one that Penny downloaded from the People Department, I suspect you will find it differs in one very small, but I would suggest very important, detail.'

Rory looked intrigued. 'In what way exactly, William?'

The vicar looked up at him. He pointed to the same line that Trevor Winter had highlighted to him just a few hours earlier.

'I rather doubt yours has this particular name on it.'

The others stared as they read the name of the man they believed to be the chief architect of the repatriation strategy.

Byron St John had been born an Outsider too.

Chapter 17

FIND THE PHOENIX

The next morning, Clarry Lionheart made his way up the hill from home in the direction of the market. His nephew, Richard – known to all for obvious reasons as Dickie – Clarry's brother having named the boy according to his sense of humour rather than with a thought for how cruel children can be to each other – was already there, working the stall.

Clarry reached the crossroads at the top of the hill, where the land flattened out to eventually become the broad, tree-lined St Peter's Street that hosted the market, and he waited as the traffic passed in front of him.

As he crossed the road, he could hear the shouts and cries of some of his equally colourful counterparts hawking their wares from their stalls.

He waved a hand in automatic acknowledgement to a call of 'Hey Clarry' from a few yards to his right and was surprised to find his arm grabbed in a friendly but excited way by the man who had greeted him.

This turned out to be 'Mad' Matty, a tall, stringy-looking individual with straggly sandy hair and a wispy beard which was teased into a ludicrous point ending just beneath his chin.

Matty had staring blue eyes which bobbed in one direction after another, which had earned him his nickname.

'Clarry! Clarry! Have you heard?' he asked earnestly, his eyes popping out from his face with its very white skin that looked stretched to its limit across his bony features.

'Hello Matty, have I heard what?' Clarry, along with everyone else on the market, was used to being asked questions by Matty – most of them of a bizarre and unexpected nature.

But this was one of those occasions when Matty – who spoke to everyone – had actually got hold of something that was interesting.

'I'm going to get some money Clarry – are you getting some? We can all have some you know!'

The big grocer, who had been continuing his walk up towards the market through a narrow street called French Row, halted and turned to face his excitable questioner.

'What money's that now Matty?' he asked, calmly.

'The money from the big city, Clarry – from the big city! We just have to tell them some names and they give us money; lots of money! I'm going to get some Clarry – are you?'

Not quite knowing how to respond to this burbling, Clarry was rather relieved when he heard the reedy voice of Dickie shouting to him from his stall farther along the road.

'C'mon uncle – I'm all on my own up here!'

He waved at Dickie and began walking again, Matty still hanging onto the arm of his coat.

'So what names do we have to tell them then Matty if we want some of this money eh?' he asked kindly.

148

'They want to know about the bombers and the snatchers Clarry! They want to know who they are – that's all; we just have to tell them, and they give us money! I'm going to tell them Clarry!' shrieked Matty, the little point of his beard waggling as he shouted.

Clarry stood stock still again, this time oblivious to the size of the crowd around his stall which Dickie was doing his best to serve with humour rather than exasperation.

His voice became serious as he turned once more to face Matty. 'Where did you hear this Matty?' he asked.

'On the market this morning – you missed them because it's Dickie's day today isn't it? But he'll tell you – you ask Dickie!'

And with this very definite instruction, Matty finally let go of Clarry's arm and danced off to engage his next conversational victim.

Dickie gave his uncle a pleading look as he reached the stall, so Clarry walked round the back and pitched in, and was up to his elbows in bananas and oranges before he could think any further.

It was only when the ten-minute rush had calmed down that he even had a chance to exchange a word with his nephew, who looked as though he had been through the wringer already.

'Sorry not to get here sooner Dickie; I got stopped by Mad Matty on my way up – he was banging on about being given money by The City of all things – what is he like, I ask you!'

'Well, he's a loon isn't he uncle, but he's right this time!'

'What do you mean, he's right this time?'

'Well, I dunno if you heard but someone blew up a shop the

other night – apparently it was owned by The City – and whoever this was kidnapped some girl the police had taken there and then firebombed the place, with two policemen stuck inside it!

'I thought it was quite funny meself but there were a couple of blokes from The City here this morning when we were setting up and they're going round offering big rewards for information on who did it. It's so much money it'll tempt anyone who knows anything. Though I doubt if Matty will be able to get much from them – he'll probably tell 'em it was you, uncle!'

Clarry forced out a laugh. 'Ha! Yes, I'd better be on my guard!'

The grocer turned to shift a crate of oranges, knowing he had never said a truer word in jest.

Exe drove through the suburbs in the direction of The City; he was doing what he termed 'routine reconnaissance' to check on the condition of some of the routes he used regularly when he was making his way into or out of the metropolis on his raids.

He had realised long ago that such diligence was vital to his attempt to stay one step ahead of The City authorities and had played no small part in his never having been caught or having had his face added to the criminal databases.

The closest that had ever come to happening was when Rory had rescued him from the two police officers in his old home – they had seen him, could describe him and probably identify him if they saw him again – but they didn't know his name or have any pictures of him.

Exe knew that the day that happened his chances of continuing his successful raids would be reduced from slim to zero.

Not knowing how long his partnership with Rory would last, this was not a chance he was prepared to take, hence his driving around the fringes of the motorway rim, visiting apparently random out of the way spots.

As he was about to pull away from one of these, Exe looked up at the sky and watched as a series of drones appeared to the south. They were quickly above him, their little blue lights clearly flashing, before passing overhead without either slowing down or stopping.

Exe breathed a sigh of relief. Then he looked up again and saw another set coming from the same direction. And then there was another; until wave after wave of police drones from The City had gone over, all in the direction of the Outside.

He pursed his lips in thought. Clearly, he wasn't the only one doing some reconnaissance today.

Clarry had left Dickie to set up the stall on his own that morning because it was his daughter Lily's first day in her new job in The City. Like any proud father, Clarry had been keen to see her off with a word or two of wisdom and a huge hug, out of which the skinny girl had managed to wriggle eventually.

When she returned home that evening, she was ready to tell all about her first day and started with the excitement that getting on the train had provided before she even left the Outside.

She told her listening parents: 'So, when I got to the barriers, there were all these staff there from The City, including that Mr Edgeley who came to interview me.

'They were double-checking every single worker's paperwork,

making them show their identification, their work permit everything. Of course, I assumed this was normal, but everyone said it wasn't, that they normally just passed through using their green cards. It held up the whole train for ages – no-one could understand what was going on.

'Then when I got through the barriers, I realised why. There were more of them on the platform, all going round giving out these leaflets,' – she handed one over to Clarry and Ruth – 'and there were copies of them put up as posters on the inside of every window on the train too. What do you think of that then?' she asked, the excitement causing her voice to rise as she finished speaking.

Clarry looked down at the piece of printed paper in his hand. It read: 'WANTED: For attempted murder, kidnap, arson and theft: £10,000 reward for information leading to the identification and capture of Outsider known as The Phoenix'. Beneath this were contact methods for informers to use.

Lily went on: 'People were saying they wished they knew who this man was – because if they were going to be held up like this every day while the police are looking for him, they'd rather dob him in! Can you believe that?'

Ruth was also reading the leaflet. 'Well,' she said, sliding a glance at her husband who sat next to her, 'fancy that.'

Looking back to her daughter, she asked: 'And how was the rest of your day darling?'

Lily then held forth for half an hour on the sights and sounds of The City she had been able to take in, between her rounds of cleaning.

Clarry, having noted the fact that the two policemen had managed to escape alive from the blaze in the clock shop, pretended to listen whilst hoping desperately that Rory was getting on quickly with the plan he had outlined to the others after they had discovered the bombshell news about Byron St John the night before.

He need not have worried. That same morning Rory had been up unusually early for him and, having paid a call on Roger to give him his instructions, drove to the outskirts of town to a grey industrial estate to put into action the second part of the scheme he had devised.

His car jolted down the road that pierced the estate, its surface rutted and pitted from years of over-use by heavy lorries. Rory steered erratically from left to right to avoid the worst of the potholes.

He pulled into the parking area in front of a printworks halfway up the road. This itself was part gravel, part dust.

Ignoring the main entrance, Rory walked down the left-hand side of the building and around the back until he saw the open, rolled-up shutters of a loading bay that had been described to him.

As he approached, a small forklift was being driven out slowly, carrying a large pile of cardboard boxes, held together by blue strapping.

Rory waited until the little truck had gone past before entering through the loading bay doorway.

'Can I help you mate?' asked a heavily-built, balding man,

who had just finished talking to a thin-faced colleague in his 50s with a thick head of wiry, ginger hair.

'I hope so,' replied Rory. 'I'm looking for Bill – I have an appointment with him.'

'Fine,' said the man, 'and which Bill would that be then? We have two of them,' he added, by way of explanation.

'Ah,' said Rory, realising why the name he had been given sounded a little odd. 'It's Copper Bill I'm looking for.'

The man with the wiry ginger top looked up. 'That's me – Copper Bill,' he said. 'You'll be Rory then I take it?' and when the visitor nodded, the printer continued: 'Come with me then, and we'll see what we can do for you.'

Chapter 18

THE NOISE

The day after Rory's visit to the printworks, Exe drove him towards The City.

'You sure about this?' the driver asked.

Rory's laugh was a slightly nervous one.

'Sure? No, but I think it's necessary. I've been away six months and a lot can change there in that time. They're constantly building, changing road layouts, things like that, and I'd hate for something to go wrong just because I hadn't prepared properly.'

Exe nodded. As someone who also believed in advance planning, he understood. On balance, he too felt that making this visit was a gamble worth taking.

Rory was confident he would not be picked up by security cameras once they were inside; he was believed to be dead, so wouldn't be on the 'watch' database which could lead to his presence being detected.

Even if he was on the list, he hoped that the alterations made to his face during his plastic surgery might be sufficient to fool the cameras, even if they wouldn't stop him being recognised in the flesh by anyone who actually knew him personally.

But he had insisted Penny stay behind at the Station House

because he felt sure she would be at risk.

It was gone 9pm and already dark. They passed through the quiet and dreary outlying suburbs which, now more than ever, formed such an uninspiring hinterland between the rich and the poor.

Rory looked through the windscreen. Ahead of them, before they would reach The City limits, was The Clearance area.

Before his Removal, Rory had been told in confidence by one of his contacts that the land was eventually going to be built on to expand The City – and his informant had said that the next swathe of inner suburbs would then also be knocked down in their turn and more people displaced, to maintain the distance between the enlarged City and the Outside.

For now, the section they were driving through lay largely empty, with nature beginning to slowly reclaim its remaining streets. A few small tented villages had grown up in places where buildings had already been demolished, though these too were cleared whenever The City authorities felt like doing so.

Exe turned off the main road, reducing his speed as they drove along what was now no more than a gently undulating track which took them further towards City territory.

A mile ahead of them everything changed, and a wall of light filled their vision. The difference between the silent, sleeping suburbs they had just driven through and this lit-up urban playground was stark and over-powering.

A row of old-fashioned, two-storey terraced houses lay directly in front of them, and Exe pulled the car over by them.

Rising above their red-tiled rooftops was The City.

High rise building after high rise building competed to dominate its neighbours, all failing because none had space to breathe, let alone command their surroundings.

Even from there, they could see the ever-changing advertising messages screaming out from the electronic billboards, grinding the consumer message into even the most hardened of heads.

And with the light came the noise.

Exe pressed a button inside the car to lower the driver's window. At once, a crushing rush of sound hit them. It was a potent mixture of the low, constant electronic whine of the little Buzzer cars that swept the Citizens through the streets that were like furred-up arteries; the clanging advertising slogans emanating from the billboards which could speak as well as blind; and the sheer hubbub created by the crowds to whom a good night out was a daily essential rather than an occasional treat.

Exe looked across at Rory as he raised the window and turned off the engine.

'Missed it, Rory?'

The smile that played on Rory's face was lethal in its insincerity. 'Like you wouldn't believe,' he answered.

They got out of the car, which Exe had been careful to leave in the pool of darkness by the small houses which dwelt in the shadows of this light fantastic.

Rory moved off in front, guiding them through street after vivid street.

As he walked, he felt as though his insides were being shaken around by the noise which just a short time ago had seemed normal to him. It was incredible, he thought, how just a few months out of this madness turned one's expectations of the world upside down.

His eyes flickered to the left, to the right and then back ahead of him; he was half fearful that he would be recognised by someone he had known, but the masses of people hemming them in from all sides barely gave them a glance as they travelled, as though on invisible tracks, in pursuit of the next passing thrill.

Inside, Rory felt cold; he hated the non-stop noise of the nightlife that surrounded him; of the adverts constantly shrieking their soulless promises at him.

Even when he had lived in The City, he had done his best to avoid these night-time scrums.

He had never felt the need to prove himself a social animal night after night and the serious nature of his work at the Daily gave him a reasonable excuse to keep away from the worst of their excesses.

Once more, as he led the way through the intricate maze of streets that had been created by the constant building upwards of steel, glass and concrete, Rory found himself considering his outsider status.

During his unexpectedly shortened journalistic career he had always felt like an observer rather than an active participant.

Now that he was back treading The City streets again having experienced a different way of life, that feeling was magnified a thousand-fold.

They continued to manoeuvre through the heaving crowds until Rory was stopped in his tracks when a particularly rowdy group jostled past them and he felt a hand in his back shoving him forward so that he almost fell into a large young man with floppy blond hair who was towards the rear of the group.

'Watch where you're going!' the man shouted directly into Rory's face, his staring eyes and the alcohol on his breath causing Rory to inadvertently flinch.

'What's your problem?' he shouted again, his face getting even nearer as he sensed Rory's discomfort. Rory put up his hands to try to make peace but the younger man, in his high and drunken fug, misinterpreted the gesture and went to take a swing at Rory, who was only saved by Exe grabbing hold of the man's forearm before he could connect.

'On your way,' said Exe, 'someone just pushed him into you – nothing's happening here.'

For a moment Rory thought Exe had miscalculated but another of the man's companions hustled him away before any further damage could be done and within seconds the danger had passed, along with the tail-end of the group, two of whom jeered and gesticulated as they went by.

'Thanks,' muttered Rory, 'nice here, isn't it?'

Exe laughed. 'Trust me, it's better than a lot of estates on the Outside I could take you to.'

They walked on, doing their best to avoid more groups tacking drunkenly from side to side on their way to the next bar.

All around them, the noise continued.

Metallic voices blared from the advertising billboards; music videos banged away on big screens, their beats shaking the buildings they were attached to; car horns from the Buzzers honked as passengers recognised acquaintances on the street; and hundreds of shrill voices created a head-high tidal wave of uninhibited sound that scrambled Rory's senses.

After what seemed to him like hours, he and Exe turned a corner into a street that was finally quieter and he stopped opposite an aggressive 20-storey building made of black glass.

As they watched the Buzzers being kept the regulation distance apart by their sensors, Rory pointed up to the signage of the City Daily.

'I thought this would be a suitable spot to start,' he said as Exe laughed. 'And everything looks exactly as it was here, so let's head off to the other places I have in mind – they're all within walking distance.'

They carried on, following's Rory's rudimentary drawn map – he had decided not to use any online mapping service in case they were later traced.

As they made their way between two of the locations he wanted to visit, he took a short cut down a narrow street formed by towers of steel and glass that climbed towards the clouds.

At the end of it, they turned into a little mews which appeared to be a dead end.

'Rory?' Exe queried, one eyebrow rising slightly. 'Are you sure this is the right way?'

'Yes, follow me,' replied Rory and walked towards a wooden door to the right-hand side of the brick wall that seemed to cut them off from making any further progress.

On the other side of the door, they found themselves in a fine garden square. Rory led the way along a path on the right and towards another, similar, door on the far side.

Remarkably, inside this little urban oasis, Exe was amazed to notice it was quiet; almost silent.

'This is uncanny,' he said.

Rory nodded. 'It's a real retreat amongst all this craziness. I discovered it once while out on a story. I think it was about the only place I ever found within The City that was properly peaceful, though I guess the churches might have offered that once – before they were demolished or repurposed.

'Now I know that I can feel this way every day if I want to.'

They walked on through the square. Rory opened the second door on the other side of it and all the noise of The City's nightlife struck them once again and those few seconds of tranquillity were ripped away as though they could never have existed.

Within an hour they had visited all the places Rory had identified. Exe made notes as they went along, carefully checking entrances, exits and alternative escape routes.

The two of them began their walk back to where they had left the car, taking a different route to the way they had come but still sticking as much as possible to roads in and around the night-time quarter.

Although it was a longer way round, leaving them to once again run the gauntlet of the revellers, it also meant they wouldn't stick out on CCTV cameras in the way they would if they were walking down otherwise empty streets in the business district at this time of the night.

They eventually reached the small row of two-storey homes they had parked by on the fringe of The City.

Rory could not understand how those houses were still standing when all around them were ever-rising monuments to greed and good living, but he was thankful, even as a former Citizen now, that places like this little row and the silent garden square had survived – at least until now.

He was sure it would only be a matter of time, but it seemed 'progress' still had some outliers left to lay waste to.

They got into the car. Exe swiftly moved off, without lights, as he followed one of his chosen routes out through the suburbs and back to the Outside.

At one point, he thought they had been spotted by a drone, so he hid the car in the deep, dark shadows of a small copse by the roadside for 15 minutes before he started for home again.

Chapter 19

DEATH ON THE TRACK

Barnaby Edgeley was an unmemorable man largely because he went out of his way to be unmemorable. He dressed averagely, had his hair cut averagely and went to great pains to remain in the background as much as possible.

If he was in a crowd, you wouldn't spot him. And if you did happen to see him walking down the street alone, you would struggle to recall any real detail about him afterwards.

Barnaby Edgeley liked it that way.

The day after Rory and Exe's City visit he received a message from police surveillance headquarters, as a result of routine drone reconnaissance. He was told to check out within 24 hours what appeared to be a disused railway station, to where a car that had been travelling from just outside City territory the night before had been trailed.

Security had been stepped up during the search for the Outsider who had hijacked a Removal and fire-bombed one of The City's holding houses and these call-outs were to be expected until someone was caught.

That evening, Edgeley sighed and put on his coat. As an afterthought he went to the desk in the small room of his flat that he used as a study and took out his gun. Other than firing range practice he had never used it and he hated the idea of ever having to do so, but his position in the People Department was a cover for his main task of being Richard Brown's eyes and ears out here, and that role required more than paperclips and box files, whether he liked it or not.

He left his flat in Tankerfield Place, opposite the cathedral, a development The City now owned, unbeknown to most of its tenants, and got into his car before driving through the dark, quiet and largely empty town centre and out in the direction of the location he had been given.

As he approached it and brought his car to a halt, he felt inside his jacket for the small gun, and shivered.

Exe was first to reach the screen inside the Station House when the alarm was triggered.

Rory and Penny were not far behind.

Seeing the area that was lit up on the screen, Exe selected the cameras that covered that section of the station, which featured sheds that had once housed everything from coal to locomotives and other rolling stock.

Most had now been converted to different uses more relevant to Rory's requirements.

Exe soon spotted the shape of a person despite the darkening evening.

'That's Edgeley...' breathed Rory, recognising the man he and Exe had followed from Clarry's house after his interview with young Lily.

'Hell Rory, how did he find us?' asked Exe.

Rory shook his head. 'I don't know but it's not altogether a surprise. The City has really been stepping up its efforts over the last couple of days.'

Something struck him then. 'It's interesting that no other alarms are going; it looks like he's alone.'

Exe nodded. 'Maybe he's just looking us over. We don't really want him reporting back to anyone though, do we?'

Agreeing, Rory leaned across and flicked a switch on the board next to the screen.

'That's blocked the phone signals, so he won't be calling anyone while he's here. That gives us a bit of time to see what he's up to.'

The three of them watched to see where Edgeley went next. They saw him creep between two of the sheds, and peer into the small, narrow reinforced window of the one that 'Just Stella' worked in. Rory knew he wouldn't be able to see anything of importance from there and was pleased he had installed such strong locks as he watched the man try unsuccessfully to open the door.

Edgeley continued to move slowly around the sheds, trying the doors on two more of them, only to find they too were locked. He looked across the rail line in the direction of the Station House and signal box, at which point Rory decided to act.

'Let's get out there and see what his game is,' he said and gave the others instructions as they quietly let themselves out through a side door.

They fanned out to their positions around the station.

Crouching down, Edgeley was now making slow and careful progress towards the platform and the Station House.

Penny was approaching from that direction while the others were circling round behind Edgeley. She reached and hid behind a lone train carriage that stood in front of a low, flatbed goods wagon on the spur from the main line that ended in a set of buffers.

Then she heard a scuffling noise and a triumphant shout from farther along the spur. She took six quick steps towards the corner of the carriage and looked down the line.

To her horror she saw Edgeley standing over a prone Exe, a gun in The City man's right hand. Exe was half lying, half sitting on the sleeper in between the two rails. Even in the gloom, Penny could see the look of utter disgust on his face as he realised he had been caught.

Then she heard Rory's voice from behind Exe. 'Leave him be, Edgeley. It's me you're looking for.'

The man with the gun took a step back to move out of range in case Exe should decide to try to disarm him and looked up at Rory. He was shocked to hear his own name used and his excitement at the fact that his apparently routine mission had taken an unexpected turn led his normally quiet, smooth voice to fray at the edges as he suddenly had an inspiration.

'You're The Phoenix, aren't you?' he shouted.

'If that's what you want to call me,' replied Rory. 'The man you're pointing that gun at certainly isn't, so let him go.'

'It's not that simple,' said Edgeley, whose nerves were causing his voice to operate at such a higher pitch than usual that he barely recognised it as his own.

'I can't go back without you, and I guess you're not going to let me take both of you very easily, are you?'

Rory could guess what was in the panicking man's mind even before he saw Edgeley's arm straighten.

But Penny had guessed too. She crept round the front of the carriage, reached the goods wagon, released its brake lever and shoved with everything she had so it set off down the slight incline of the line.

Barnaby Edgeley heard a creaking noise from behind him, followed by a low rumble and then a woman's voice which shouted 'Exe, jump!'

The man from the People Department would not have been human if he hadn't turned his head in the direction of the shout, but all he could see was a dark mass gathering pace towards him down the line. He stumbled in his panic and the goods wagon was upon him.

Penny's shout and Exe's alacrity meant the skinny thief leapt to safety with a second to spare. Penny and Rory were at his side by the time the goods wagon that had run over the unnoticeable Barnaby Edgeley had crashed into the buffers with a grinding smash.

Together, they walked back up the line. There was nothing they could do for Edgeley.

Chapter 20

READ ALL ABOUT IT

'Dr' Johnson, that veteran if unlikely Health Correspondent of the City Daily, squeezed himself with difficulty into the black Buzzer that he found waiting on the corner of Fleet Street.

He tapped his phone on the dashboard to close the doors, start up the electric engine and pay, then typed in the address of the restaurant where he was due to meet one of his contacts for what promised to be an excellent lunch.

Taking one of the individual, self-driving small cars that you could pick up in any street in The City wasn't the easiest thing to do for a man of Johnson's size but compared with the alternative of descending underground and suffering sharing a Tube carriage with so many other people dashing here, there and everywhere for whatever (and sometimes no) reason, it was infinitely preferable.

It had the added attraction of enabling him to shut out the cacophony outside. Inside the little cabin on wheels, he could choose to enjoy rather more soothing sounds on his journey, read an e-book or watch a video on the screen.

But because news was his stock in trade, he opted instead to tap into the live news feed that his own paper provided, so he was as up to date as possible with what was going on before his meeting.

As he sought out the headlines, his Buzzer turned the corner into High Holborn and Johnson looked up at the ever-changing electronic billboards that disfigured so many of the grand buildings.

The news feed spluttered into life inside the Buzzer and as it did so he noticed a change in the advertising messages which all suddenly flashed up the same message:

'BREAKING NEWS... BREAKING NEWS...'

His news feed inside the Buzzer was now showing the very same alert.

The journalist concentrated on the small screen in front of him in the Buzzer's dashboard.

'Minister guilty of mass social cleansing – Byron St John is an Outsider,' read the headline that ticker-taped across.

Johnson sat back as far as he could in the tiny capsule, his eyes wide open as he watched the headline repeated on the screen in front of him.

Then a voice cut in: 'Attention all Citizens! Attention all Citizens! We can today reveal that Byron St John, the Deputy Finance Director, has been pursuing a policy of illegally Removing people who were secretly brought into The City as children a generation ago to live and work here. We can also tell you that this is despite Byron St John being born an Outsider himself...'

Just as the story was getting going, the screen in front of Johnson went dark and, at the same time, the electronic signs all along the road did the same, as, for the first time he could remember, the journalist found his senses were no longer being assaulted with promotional messages.

That was odd enough, he thought. But what was even stranger was that he thought he recognised the voice that had made the startling accusations against one of The City's most influential leaders.

It sounded just like one of his former colleagues at the Daily, who had disappeared most unexpectedly just a matter of months ago. He could have sworn that voice had belonged to Rory Kennet.

As the screens went blank, a gang of teenage boys with cloth caps pulled down over their faces emerged from the back of a white van with false number plates that was driven into Trafalgar Square.

Dispersing quickly, they each ran to a different nearby street, carrying large canvas bags over their shoulders.

As they ran, each of them shouted: 'Read all about it – Byron St John's an Outsider!' as they pulled printed sheets of paper from their bags and thrust them into the hands of every astonished Citizen they came across.

In different parts of The City, including right outside the offices of the Daily, the same scene played out; multiple vans disgorging a group of fleet-footed street urchins with obscured faces shouting the news and forcing the printed papers on as many people as possible.

They continued, accosting unsuspecting Citizens going about their normal business, until they had distributed them all, and then they swarmed back into the vans which screeched out of The City using tactics and routes that had been prescribed in advance by Exeter Pikey.

'What is this?' cried one man who had found his hitherto empty right hand was suddenly filled with the latest sensation.

'It's called a newspaper,' cried the newsboy in delight as he ran towards his next customer. 'Read all about it, mister…!'

'Dunwoody.' The woman's brittle, clipped voice echoed down the phone that the Reverend William Faraday was holding.

'Millie? It's William Faraday,' he said.

After a moment's pause, the woman replied. 'William! Interesting timing – I take it you've heard what's going on?'

'Actually, it's why I'm ringing,' said the vicar.

'That's more and more interesting,' said Millicent Dunwoody, the private secretary to the Lord Mayor of The City.

'I thought you might say that. I'll get straight to the point. I know who is behind this and the only way it's going to be resolved is if the Lord Mayor himself gets involved. Can you arrange a private meeting?'

Miss Dunwoody exhaled noticeably. 'William, are you sure about this? He's incredibly busy and this whole thing has caused a proper stir. You know they've even declared an emergency Bank Holiday to take the people's minds off it?'

William chortled. 'I know – I hear it's being called Byron Day in some quarters!'

The woman laughed back. 'Yes – I believe so. I'm not sure that's quite what was intended but there you go. OK, tell me what it is you need, and I'll talk to him straight away.'

The vicar told his old friend what he wanted and added some conditions: that the meeting would be held at his church; that the government's leader himself was to come, with just one or two of his key people, and that there should be no attempt to apprehend anyone who attended, before, at or after the meeting.

After some discussions throughout the day the meeting was agreed.

William later confided in Rory that this was not the first time he had acted as a go-between or, as he preferred to describe it, an 'honest broker' when there had been problems to resolve between The City and the Outside.

Rory was becoming used to being surprised by William, but he still questioned how many more unexpected revelations the churchman would have for him.

Even now, as he prepared for the meeting with the most powerful man in The City, he wasn't sure that William had told him everything about how and why he had left his previous life behind – or whether he truly had done – but he instinctively trusted that the vicar was on his side.

Chapter 21

AFTER THE FUNERAL

The funeral cortége wound its way around the silent, suburban streets, sleepy in the heat haze that shimmered above the baking Tarmac on this unexpectedly hot autumn day.

As inexorable as death itself, it reached the gates of St Peter's Church, in advance of a ceremony in a churchyard where the lack of grave space meant no-one had been buried for 50 years.

The mourners were an odd-looking bunch too, as anyone who cared to look closely would have noticed. For a start they were all men. And they were all men chosen for their physical attributes. They were either big, strong and hefty or small, strong and wiry. They were all able to fight, and most were well able to run too. They had been hand-picked for the occasion by the recruitment agency of Lionheart and Pikey.

On the corners of every street approaching the church, more men and women were posted. All were watching and waiting for one vehicle that, in keeping with the occasion, would almost certainly be large, black and limousine-like.

But it was not the hearse.

For that had already stopped outside the gate of St Peter's and the funeral attendants slowly and carefully (just in case anyone was watching) removed the coffin from the back of the vehicle.

It was a cheap, thin casket; of the type chosen by those who had no money. Or those who simply didn't care. But the organisers had at least gone to the trouble and expense of having a brass plaque engraved and screwed into the coffin lid.

It read: 'The Political Career of Byron St John'.

Ten minutes after the procession had gathered round a patch of ground which already played host to three generations of one family placed reverently on top of each other, the message went round that the vehicle of honour was approaching the church. The watchers on the street corners were doing their job.

The crowd around the graveside of Byron St John's leadership aspirations moved into line to shield the ceremony from prying eyes. When the car arrived, all its occupants saw was a wall of black-dressed backs.

A large man in a tight-fitting charcoal suit, whose broad shoulders and shaven bullet head gave him the unmistakeable air of a security officer, got out of the car first, enabling two other men and one woman to do so next.

They were met by the swirling cassock of the out-rushing Reverend William Faraday, whose more formal clerical attire was designed to assist with the impression of a funeral.

The vicar shook the hand of a tall, scholarly looking man with a long thin face, silver-grey hair and notable black eyebrows. 'Welcome Mr Lord Mayor, it is so nice to see you again,' he said.

Sir Jonty Knight, the head of The City's government, acknowledged the welcome and murmured something civil in reply.

William moved on to shake the hand of the woman, who was

short and slightly overweight. She had a shrewd piercing look that sidled down her long, thin nose that ended in wildly flaring nostrils.

She took a quick glance over her shoulder and said, in an incredulous tone of voice: 'Do you still put them in the ground out here then?'

William retrieved his hand from her professionally perfunctory grip. His eyes twinkled as he replied: 'Well, this one was from an old Outsider family, you know.'

The Lord Mayor said: 'Reverend William Faraday, meet Marsha Field. Marsha is our new Finance Director; the previous incumbent having been replaced – partly because of the reason we are here with you today – he apparently failed to notice what his deputy was up to.'

'Ah yes, indeed,' said William, 'Were you not in charge of the People Department before, Ms Field?'

The woman stared down her nose again. 'I was, yes,' she said shortly, with no interest.

William ignored the snub and turned instead to also welcome the Head of the Civil Service, Sir Anthony Brotherton, a tidy little man who dressed as though it was the 1950s.

He ushered the visitors into the church.

At that exact moment, the mourners left the graveside of another failed politician's ambitions and gathered by the main entrance to the churchyard, cutting off The City leaders' car, much to the silent consternation of its driver.

Half the men and women who had been on alert duty around the streets had now made their way to the church and they split up to guard the alternative routes into the grounds, whilst others stayed in place ready to pass the word in case any more cars from The City should suddenly appear.

Rory had taken no chances when agreeing to this meeting with the heads of the government and the fake funeral was his way of ensuring he was surrounded with very useful help should he need it, as well as a convenient way of disposing of the body of Mr Barnaby Edgeley.

William led the Lord Mayor, the Finance Director and the Head of the Civil Service down the nave and off towards one of the side rooms of his church.

As the government party approached the door, William barred the way with his arm to stop the security guard coming in first, and said: 'Sorry, we have agreed on no security or police presence within the meeting itself.'

The Lord Mayor nodded. 'It's quite all right Thompson – that is what we agreed, and I have very good reason to trust the vicar.'

The government trio entered the room, followed by William, who promptly removed his clerical outerwear to reveal his usual trim suit.

The vicar closed the door behind them. They looked around and saw... no-one.

William indicated three chairs which were ranged all on one side of the large table that sat in the middle of the room. 'Please do sit down,' he said.

The Lord Mayor's long face had a look which was half query, half frown. 'Are we expecting a grand entrance?' he asked, as he took a seat, followed by the others.

The Reverend William Faraday shook his head slowly. 'Not exactly,' he replied, as he picked up a remote control from the table.

On the other side of the table was a large screen which flickered into life a second after the vicar touched a button.

A colourful graphic of a bird rising from the ashes appeared on the screen, immediately followed by an avatar depicting a man with a prominent jaw and flaming red hair. Jolly Roger had been creatively busy.

The avatar spoke.

'Thank you for coming, and please do not hold it against the vicar that I am not with you in person. I am sure you will understand the need for me to protect my identity at this stage. Please address the screen directly when we have this discussion – I can see you all from where I am.'

The Lord Mayor looked a little disconcerted. Marsha Field looked livid. Sir Anthony Brotherton remained utterly unmoved, his face completely tranquil. William stood to the right-hand side of the table, watching all three of them.

It was Sir Jonty Knight who replied.

'I understand your reticence, though it is unnecessary. Just to be clear, although I think it is now obvious, our security reports have identified a man who is wanted for questioning about two serious incidents that have involved The City. This man is apparently known by an alias, or nickname, of The Phoenix. I take it that is you?'

'It's not a name of my own choosing, but it's one that has been applied to me,' Rory admitted. 'There is a reason for it, which I think rather apt, but I won't be going into that with you today. I am here to discuss your government's Removals policy for all the Outsiders who were taken to live in The City when they were children.'

The silver-haired politician looked at the screen sharply. 'It was not my government's policy; of that I can assure you. These were the actions of a few rogue ministers and officials whose loyalties became somewhat blurred and misplaced. I would like to apologise for what happened and make it clear that The Board's view is those events should never have taken place.'

Avatar Rory remained polite but was unconvinced. 'You must remember that the consequences of this policy – whether it was official or not – have been life-changing for thousands of innocent people.

'And for what? To satisfy the cock-eyed whim of a small number of highly privileged, incompetent and quite possibly corrupt politicians.'

An uncomfortable look spread across the Lord Mayor's face but Rory enjoyed more the blazing anger that briefly pierced the mask of the newly promoted Finance Director. His knowledge of her previous role did little to reassure him of her goodwill.

'Perhaps we should move the conversation on,' Marsha Field almost hissed at the Lord Mayor.

She turned back to on-screen Rory.

'Your newspaper stunt was childish and, although it may have caused a little stir for a short while, it will do no lasting damage,' she said.

The avatar smiled.

'So why are you here then?'

Marsha Field spluttered and Rory, who was nearby in a room elsewhere in the church, could have sworn he saw the ghost of a smile flit momentarily across the lips of the Lord Mayor before the curiously retro Sir Anthony Brotherton interjected in a carefully modulated voice.

'Regardless of the success or otherwise of your attempt to disrupt life in The City on this occasion, The Board has no wish to continue a feud with you, or to fuel any further discontent among those who live on the Outside.

'The Lord Mayor has already explained that this unfortunate policy of forced Removal of those who had been brought into The City was not official, and that it was carried out by rogue elements. The government has taken steps to ensure closer scrutiny of ministers and their immediate entourages so that no such deviations can happen again.

'We would very much like you to accept this fact, and to desist from pursuing this matter further.'

The poisonous Ms Field then did her best to undermine the placid civil servant's good work.

'If you don't agree, you won't find it so easy to project your messages to the Citizens again anyway. We have improved the security of our systems since your stunt.'

Rory's avatar spoke. 'Have you now? Let's see how successful you have been then, shall we?'

The red-haired graphic dissolved from the screen and in its place was the unmistakable view of Westminster. The screen zoomed in on the electronic advertising billboards that were set along the row of buildings opposite The City's seat of government.

On each of them, a clip was showing a live feed from the room they were in right now. Rory's avatar appeared in the bottom right-hand corner of the screen, waving. Then the screens went blank for five seconds before a moving illustration of a small bird rising from the ashes was shown on repeat.

They cut out again for a further five seconds, before an advert for a holiday to the Maldives flashed up, signalling that life in The City had returned to normal.

Marsha Field's face went from pale to flushed, but she kept her mouth closed. The Lord Mayor and the Head of the Civil Service looked at each other.

Sir Jonty Knight smoothed his right eyebrow as Rory's avatar reappeared on the screen across the table from him.

'Just what is it you want out of all this?' he asked. 'I can tell you already that Byron St John has been removed from his position on The Board – and Removed from The City as well. I am hoping that will satisfy at least one of your demands.'

'It does, but it is the least I would have expected you to say – and do. I think it must be clear to you by now that we are able to get our messages to every Citizen in a short period of time. And you know as well as I do that it won't take too long for a few similar stunts – as Ms Field calls them – to begin to erode trust in your government and embolden those who may wish to change the status quo.

'If you want to avoid that happening, I also want every

Outsider-Citizen who was Removed under this policy offered the opportunity to return should they wish to do so. If they do not wish to, they should be entitled to a much higher resettlement grant to give them a chance of starting a new and comfortable life on the Outside – say ten times the current grant you give to those who volunteer to leave.'

Rory could almost see the pound signs whirring through Marsha Field's dark and glowering eyes.

Sir Jonty Knight raised one of his remarkable eyebrows and said, quietly: 'Anything else?'

'Yes, two other things. Firstly, I want to know what happened to a clerk in the People Department called Lorna Sexton, who appears to have been Removed nearly six months ago. Assuming she is to be found, I want the same offer to be extended to her – and to Penny Neave who, as you know, I rescued from your thugs.'

Recoiling at this last word, the Lord Mayor nonetheless nodded. 'You said two other things.'

'I did. I want your absolute guarantee that all the Outsider-Citizens who choose to return to The City are never subjected to the threat of Removal on any grounds whatsoever in the future.'

'But that would be impossible – it would give them a different status to other Citizens,' said Sir Anthony Brotherton.

'Isn't that precisely what they have had already, without even knowing it?' retorted Rory.

Sir Jonty Knight calmly stroked his right eyebrow again.

'If we were to agree to these demands of yours, you will agree to let this current matter lie?'

'You have my word.'

The Lord Mayor looked across the table directly at the screen. 'And you know that if you break it, The City will track you down. And it won't be kind to you.'

Rory had the bizarre notion that the warning was intended to be friendly, rather than threatening.

Through his avatar he returned the leader's gaze and said, simply: 'I know.'

The silver-grey head turned to the Reverend William Faraday. 'I'm sure you won't mind if the three of us go to another room to discuss this, William.' He indicated the screen. 'Preferably one that doesn't have hidden cameras and microphones recording every word.'

The vicar, standing up, had the grace to look very slightly abashed. 'Follow me,' he said.

Chapter 22

LORNA

Lorna Sexton was no longer missing. She had been released from a prison house on the personal say-so of the Lord Mayor of The City, having been held on a charge of treason.

The City's laws allowed for anyone so accused to be detained without trial for up to a year if a government minister signed off approval of the continued detention every three months. Byron St John had done so twice.

One week after the meeting between Rory, through his avatar, and the heads of The City's government, Lorna was sitting in a side room at St Peter's Church with her old friend Penny by her side, along with Rory, Exe, Clarry, Roger and, of course, the Reverend William Faraday.

Rory looked across the table at her; a woman he had met only once until today, yet who had had such a profound influence on the future course of his life.

A woman he had nearly died because of.

She was 5ft 3ins tall and pleasingly plump, with shoulder-length strawberry-blonde hair and a pleasantly attractive face with blue eyes. She looked a little tired and drawn but otherwise physically well. The mental scars, of course, he could not see.

William Faraday, that vicar who truly moved in mysterious ways, had arranged this meeting.

Though, for reasons he kept to himself, he trusted the Lord Mayor's word, he still chose to hold the reunion at his own church rather than risk taking Lorna to the Station House.

Having caught up privately first with Penny, Lorna sat down to explain what had happened to her.

'Things had been going really well for me,' she said, 'and I was earmarked for promotion which would have meant I would be entrusted with even more important and confidential work.

'It was around this time that I first met Richard Brown. I was told he was a visiting official from the Department of Finance. He seemed to take a liking to me and as I saw more of him he told me that he actually worked on special projects across different departments and that his work often took him to the Outside as well.

'After a few months my promotion came through and I was asked to sign the Official Secrets Act because of the nature of the work I was to undertake next. And that's where things started to go wrong.

'Penny says you know about The Shortage and the children who were taken to The City.'

The others nodded to confirm.

She continued: 'Like most Citizens I knew nothing about it until I began working on this project – Operation Cuckoo's Nest. But soon after I started, I was given a list of names of people who were to be Removed.

'Because I worked in the People Department, that wasn't a

new thing for me – I was used to dealing with Removals.

'But this was different. Firstly, there was the sheer volume of people. And then there was the fact that they were all of a similar and young age. It didn't seem plausible that these could have been part of the usual process.

'As I got more deeply into the project, I came across references to The Shortage so I researched to find out more.

'Soon, I saw some other information that had come from the Deputy Finance Director, and I was able to draw my own conclusions as to what lay behind it all.'

She paused as Rory asked her from across the table: 'You mean there's something more than we already know?'

'Yes, I think there is. I discovered that a series of major gambles had been taken with The City's finances on the Stock Exchange which hadn't come off and had left the Exchequer in much worse shape than had been expected.

'It was so bad, and the losses were so big, that there would have been an almost immediate need to put up taxes. As you know, The Board won't countenance that; it would go against every promise they have ever made to the Citizens. And heads would have had to roll too.

'So they decided instead to cut the money spent on public services. And the only way to do that without Citizens noticing a deterioration was to reduce the number of people using them. I think the early retirement scheme was launched to try to tackle this problem but because it would take time to make a difference, a decision was taken to Remove thousands of Citizens quickly as well.'

Exe asked one of his pertinent questions. 'But wouldn't that also reduce the number of people paying taxes? Surely it would be self-defeating?'

Lorna laughed. 'You would think so, wouldn't you? But since when does common sense come into it? No, everyone else would just be encouraged to work harder to increase revenues.

'And someone who knew about The Shortage, and how it had been tackled, came up with the bright idea of quietly Removing all the Outsiders who had been brought to The City as children; no matter what they had achieved, how hard they had worked or how much they had contributed to The City. Not being of founding City blood was the only thing that mattered to them.

'Because the number of people who knew about the situation was so limited, they were able to bank on there being no public outcry at the Removals, which could be done quietly and efficiently, using trumped-up charges where they felt they needed them – as I believe happened with you, Rory.'

Rory nodded. But he wanted to know more.

'Do you know how high up this went, Lorna? Was the whole government involved in it? Was it official policy?'

'I can't be absolutely sure. But I never saw any paperwork to indicate that anyone higher than Byron St John had signed off on it. I've had quite a lot of time to think about this and my own opinion is that it was pushed through on the quiet by a small number of very ambitious people who were responsible for the original gambles and were desperate to cover up their own failings.'

Rory asked: 'So do you think it could be possible that the Lord

Mayor, for example, might not have known about it until we got involved?'

'Knowing the way some of those ministers go about things, I'd say it's possible – yes,' Lorna replied.

While Rory considered the ramifications of what they had just learned, William changed the subject.

'May I ask how you came to get caught, Lorna?' he asked.

'Of course. Unfortunately, my immediate supervisor, who I thought was a friend, spotted that I had been looking into historic files that were outside of my remit and she reported it to Richard,' Lorna replied.

'He confronted me, and, although I said I just wanted to understand the background to important decisions, I don't think he trusted me.

'I think he did actually like me – but when he realised that I had seen the original list of Outsider children, that was it. Anything he felt for me meant nothing compared to the importance of covering up Byron St John's background.

'Two security officers turned up at my flat that same night and I was taken away and questioned.

'Even though I protested that I had signed the Act and wasn't going to say anything about it, that was that.

'And that's really as much as there is to tell,' she concluded, and she clasped her hands together on the table, looking round at the others.

'I'm just grateful you're here to tell it,' said Penny, softly.

Chapter 23

THE OUTSIDER

The fine detail of the agreement reached between the outlaw representative of the Outside and the head of The City government was now being put into practice.

The Outsider-Citizens were all being traced and offered an official apology for the hurt and harm caused to them. They were also being given the opportunity to return to The City. So far, some had accepted; some hadn't. Those who hadn't had been paid the higher resettlement grant that Rory had demanded.

The offer to return had also been extended to Lorna Sexton, following her release from the prison house.

To Rory's surprise, though not Penny's, Lorna had chosen to go back to The City.

William had journeyed to meet Rory, Exe and Penny at the Station House to discuss the latest progress.

He asked Rory: 'Did you ever consider revealing who you were to them, so you could have had the chance to return?'

Rory thought briefly. 'No, not really. The City believes Rory Kennet died in that car fire, and it suits me for now to keep it that way. I don't believe that if I had returned I would have been able to lead anything like a normal life. At the very least, I'm sure they would have kept a very close eye on me. And, to be honest with you, I rather want to keep an eye on them instead.

'I'm not convinced that this policy was all down to one rogue minister and a few of his cohorts – especially now we know, thanks to Lorna, about the financial mismanagement.

'There's no doubt at all in my mind that they've chosen to make St John the fall guy – though perhaps that's not surprising as he was the one born an Outsider. Don't get me wrong, I'm sure he was one of the prime movers, but I don't think it likely that he acted virtually alone.'

As Exe agreed, he continued: 'I've never for a moment bought the idea that The Board is basically benevolent. You only have to look at the way people are cast aside when their useful time is over and they threaten to become a burden. No civilised government would act like that against its own people.

'So I want to keep monitoring what's going on inside The City and work to make things better – both there and here on the Outside. And I need to be as free as possible to do that.'

William nodded before speaking again.

'And Penny... have you decided to stay here too? I understand you've been offered a very generous position back there.'

Rory gave the vicar a knowing glance, marvelling, not for the first time, at the quality of his sources.

Penny said: 'I'm with Rory on this. It's very difficult to trust anything The City says or does while it refuses to acknowledge that anyone other than Byron St John was behind the Removals. So it was an easy decision for me to stay too.'

William said: 'Well, that is good news. But in terms of your relationship with The City, do we at least have a truce for the time being?'

Rory paused.

'If we do, it's an uneasy one, William. I have little doubt that The Board will still try to track us down, even if it's only to keep us under surveillance. But as well as scrutinising The City we also have a lot of good work to do out here, to help those Outsiders who need it. And I'm determined to get on with that without being apprehended.'

'As a representative of the Church, I applaud you for doing that Rory,' replied William, quietly. 'I shall also continue to do everything I can to make sure you are left alone – using those limited contacts that I have.'

Rory looked across at the Reverend William Faraday, sitting there in his suit that fitted him almost like a second skin. He wondered again who he really was, and just what his connection with The City was now.

But he said, sincerely: 'Thank you William, I believe you will.'

Later, when William had left to return to Harrow, Exe invited Penny and Rory up to the signal box for a drink in what he now was beginning to really accept was his home.

'It's yours for as long as you want it, Exe,' Rory had again promised him.

While Exe and Penny talked downstairs, Rory stood alone, upstairs, looking out of the tall windows that afforded a panoramic view up the line, down the line and across the line.

The sun was going down and a red tinge brightened the far horizon, giving it the appearance of being on fire.

Rory wanted this moment on his own.

In truth, the decision not to pursue a return to The City had been a very simple one for him. The fact that he did not trust the government was a convenient cloak to mask his real reason for staying here.

He knew in his heart that he belonged on the Outside.

Here, he could look down from a hillside – or perhaps from a Victorian iron bridge – onto the vast, sprawling City with all its glories and its madness spread out before him.

Glories and madness that he was content to watch from afar but did not wish to be a part of.

It was on the Outside that he had risen, like Clarence Lionheart's Phoenix, from the flames that were intended to engulf him; flames fanned by a breeze from The City he had always felt apart from.

As he looked first down, and then up, the railway line that ran beneath him, he thought about where he had come from and where he was going to.

His grey-blue eyes narrowed a little and he smiled his thin-lipped smile as he spotted a City drone high up in the sky flying over the station.

He knew that his destiny still lay ahead of him. But right now Rory Kennet was just happy that he was home.

ACKNOWLEDGEMENTS

I would like to sincerely thank the following people who have helped me with this book.

Firstly, all those who gave their time to read early versions and have offered me helpful, constructive (and, I think, honest) feedback: John Bignall, Anna Burdass, Laura Lilley (without whose encouragement I would not have started writing this book), Justin Maltz, Stephen Widgery and Justine Woods (who kindly read several updates). I am hugely grateful to them all.

The artist and printmaker John Duffin honoured me by granting me permission to use one of his remarkable works for the jacket / cover. You can view his work at www.johnduffin.co.uk.

Edmond Terakopian showed both his skills and insight on my author photography which has also formed the basis of my website. Visit www.terakopian.com to see more of his work.

Sean Roper took my initial selection of John Duffin's work and turned it into the jacket / cover that I had always envisaged and hoped for.

Aaron Gransby